"Her last family member, the person she trusted most of all, had one foot out the door."

BREAKAWAY

JEFF HIRSCH

SCHOLASTIC INC.

For 39 Clues fans everywhere.
Thanks for making the new guy feel so welcome!

Library of Congress Control Number: 2013942298

ISBN 978-0-545-52142-0

10 9 8 7 6 5 4 3 2 1   14 15 16 17 18/0

Cahill kids p. 12: Ken Karp for Scholastic; Pony p. 12: Charice Silverman for Scholastic;
Dan p. 72: Ken Karp for Scholastic; Amy and Evan p. 73: Ken Karp for Scholastic;
art p. 190: SJI for Scholastic
Book design and illustrations by Charice Silverman

First edition, February 2014

Printed in China 62

Scholastic US: 557 Broadway • New York, NY 10012
Scholastic Canada: 604 King Street West • Toronto, ON M5V 1E1
Scholastic New Zealand Limited: Private Bag 94407 • Greenmount, Manukau 2141
Scholastic UK Ltd.: Euston House • 24 Eversholt Street • London NW1 1DB

CHAPTER 1

London

J. Rutherford Pierce smiled as the six mercenaries filed into his London office. Each one had been handpicked. The best of the best. Hardened soldiers who moved through their lives free of the fears and uncertainties of lesser men. And yet right now, each and every one of them was terrified. Pierce savored it. Some people liked wine. Some people liked fine food. Pierce liked fear.

Once the mercenaries were seated, Pierce pressed a button beneath his vast desk and the double doors behind them slammed shut.

"Sir," their leader began. "We—"

"Candy?"

Pierce pushed a large crystal bowl toward the edge of his desk. It was full to the top with small red, white, and blue spheres. Americandy. His newest creation and currently the fastest-selling sweet in the United States. The men looked back at him, uncertain, off balance, just as he wanted. Pierce smiled as he plucked out a red one and devoured it.

"The red is my favorite," he said. "Cherry pie. The blue is blueberry pie and the white is apple pie. Had to fudge the color on that one a bit, of course. Go on."

He pushed the bowl forward again and each man took one. Of course they did. The world was a symphony and Pierce was a conductor.

Pierce opened their action report.

"Why Turkey?" he asked.

"Sir, the guides they hired indicated that the children were looking for leopards."

"Anatolian leopards," Pierce corrected.

"Y-yes, sir," the mercenary stammered. "Anatolian leopards. Which are extinct."

"And where are they headed now?"

"They're taking a private plane, sir, but we were able to access their flight plans. Rome first and then Tunis, Tunisia."

"Why?"

"We, uh, we don't know, sir."

Pierce turned the page to a simple black-and-white map. Turkey and then Tunisia. Turkey was the site of ancient Troy while Tunis was once Carthage, one of the greatest empires the world had ever known. Coincidence? Pierce thought not. But what did it mean? Extinct animals. Vanished empires.

What are they after?

"So, can you tell me any way in which you and your men did *not* fail in your mission?"

The leader hesitated. Pierce slammed the report onto the desktop and the fearless men before him leaped back in their seats.

"Children!" Pierce thundered. "A group of children who should be home playing video games and avoiding their math homework took you on and they won. They *beat* you. Now, I'm sure you all came here expecting punishment, severe punishment, but I'm not going to punish you. In fact, I'm going to give you each two gifts."

The men, who had been staring down at the plush carpeting at their feet, looked up at him, tentative, but all breathing a little bit easier.

"The first gift," Pierce said, "is the opportunity to redeem yourselves. Would anyone like to know what the second one is?"

The men nodded dumbly. Honestly, sometimes it was like the entire world was moving in slow motion except for him. Pierce smiled.

"The second gift is motivation."

"Sir?" their leader said.

Pierce pulled a white pill out of a drawer in his desk and held it up to them.

"The candy you ate was filled with a slow-acting poison. Complete your assignment and return here to receive the antidote. If you are unable to complete your assignment, well, I imagine most of you would welcome a death of writhing agony after being bested twice by a group of children, wouldn't you?"

The double doors behind the men swung open as if by the force of Pierce's will.

"There," he said. "Consider yourself motivated. Now go!"

Once they were gone, Pierce popped the antidote into his mouth and went back to his report. *The Cahills.*

Individually, none of them would be of concern, but together . . .

Pierce smiled as the answer came to him.

He reached for his phone.

"Contact the heads of all our European media units," he ordered his assistant. "Anyone who isn't standing in front of me in one hour is fired."

Pierce hung up and sat back in his chair. He watched London race about below.

It was a city with a rich and expansive history. Shakespeare. Churchill. Isaac Newton.

And I'll be the one to wipe it all away.

CHAPTER 2

Rome. The Next Day.

Amy Cahill was running out of time.

She had managed to make it out of the airport and onto the tarmac unseen, but her pursuers were smart. It wouldn't be long before they picked up her trail. The private jet was sitting just ahead, fueled up, its engines already spinning into a high-pitched whine. She had to get on board and in the air, fast, before they saw her.

She peeked around the dumpster she was hiding behind. A few members of the ground crew milled around the plane making final preparations, but otherwise the coast was clear. Amy cinched her backpack tight and started to move.

"Amy Cahill!"

Amy flattened herself against the dumpster as the door from the airport to the runway flew open. Her pursuers were heading down the stairway and onto the tarmac.

"Amy! Where are you?"

She had to distract them. Amy spied what she needed a few steps away. She dashed out of her hiding place to grab a metal can off a shelf. She poured its contents into the dumpster, then pulled a match from her jacket pocket. The trash lit with a deep *whump*, exploding into a wall of flame. Amy put her back into the quickly warming metal and pushed.

"A-my!" someone cried in a taunting singsong. "A-my Ca-hill! Come out, come out, wherever you are."

Amy dug her sneakers into the asphalt and bore down on the dumpster, her spine burning against the hot steel, until she felt something give. The wheels squeaked and began to turn. Amy grunted and gave another push, and momentum took over. The dumpster raced out across the tarmac, the fire surging in the wind.

Gasps came from all around as the ground crew called out in frantic Italian. Her pursuers scattered, half of them running back to the terminal to get help while the others sprinted toward the dumpster. She had about two minutes of chaos. It was all she needed.

Amy bolted across the tarmac to the waiting plane. Dan and Ian were out of their seats and heading for the commotion when she ran up the stairs.

"Amy, what's going on!?" Dan asked.

"Pierce's men! Tell the pilot we have to get going!"

"But what about the others?"

"Now!"

Dan disappeared into the cockpit.

"Amy, are you all right?" Ian asked. "Was it Pierce's men? Did those ruffians hurt you?"

"I'm fine. We just need to—"

"Hey! What are you doing!?"

Amy froze, her back to the door. She slowly turned to face her pursuers.

"We were just getting snacks!"

Jonah and Jake stood at the foot of the stairs. Atticus, Pony, and Hamilton were behind them, holding up plastic bags that stretched under the weight of soda bottles, chips, pretzels, and candy.

"Don't look at me," Jake said as he led the group past her and into the plane. "I told them we had to get going."

"Little dudes can't be contained when they see snacks," Jonah said.

The boys passed Amy, dropping into their seats and pulling out snacks and video games. A din of conversation quickly filled the cabin. Ian hadn't moved from his place by the first row of seats. He was watching Amy intently, an unasked question in his eyes. The cockpit door opened again.

"Pilot says we're up in five," Dan said. "Hey, what happened to Pierce's goons?"

Amy found herself stuck for an answer, but Ian jumped in to save her.

"False alarm," he said. "Might as well get to our seats."

Amy hurried past everyone to the back of the plane.

Once the jet was airborne, she checked to make sure the boys were distracted and then pulled that morning's newspaper out of her backpack. Looking at it, she felt the same sick twist in her stomach she had when she'd first seen it at the airport newsstand.

The Cahills were the most powerful family history had ever known, but now they were up against their greatest challenge — J. Rutherford Pierce, a media tycoon with dreams of world domination. He had already manipulated a member of the Cahill family, a scientist named Sammy Mourad, to gain access to the Cahills' most closely guarded secret: a serum that granted near-superhuman strength and intelligence to anyone who took it. Amy and the others, afraid of what the serum would mean for the world in the hands of someone like Pierce, were on the trail of an antidote and had one component of it already, the whiskers of an Anatolian leopard. Only six more to go and they would stop Pierce for good.

Unfortunately, Pierce wasn't standing idly by while they searched. Not only had he sent teams of serum-enhanced mercenaries after them, he was attacking them daily in his many newspapers and television programs. At first he had contented himself with harassing Amy and Dan with dumb stories about what he called their irresponsible globe-trotting — and what they called TRYING TO SAVE THE WORLD! — or dumb gossip about Amy and Ian or Amy and Jake.

But now that had all changed. Amy lifted the

newspaper off her lap. Pierce wasn't just harassing them anymore. He was going for the throat.

"Everything okay?"

Amy jumped. Ian was leaning over the seat in front of her.

"Fine," Amy said as she hurriedly stuffed the newspaper into her backpack. "Everything's fine. Just . . . doing some research."

"Ah, well, you can never know too much," Ian said, falling into the seat across the aisle from Amy. "Speaking of which. Did you know the Avenue Habib Bourguiba in Tunis is known the world over as the Champs-Élysées of the near east? The cafés. The shops. The discos."

Amy couldn't help but laugh. "The discos? Honestly, Ian, who calls them discos anymore?"

"Well, the Tunisians, I expect," he sniffed. "So the plan is to rely on the Rosenblooms' father, then? He's a scientist of some sort?"

Amy set her backpack aside. "An archaeologist. Apparently, his passion is lost civilizations. He's in Tunis studying the Carthaginian ruins."

Amy hoped Dr. Rosenbloom would be able to help. He would certainly have his work cut out for him. Amy and Dan had found an ancient notebook left to them by Olivia Cahill, one of the founders of the Cahill family. The notebook gave instructions on how to create the antidote, but much of it was in code. Atticus and Jake's analysis of Olivia's notes made them certain that the next piece of the antidote was a plant native to the area around Tunisia, called silphium. Of course, because nothing was ever easy, silphium was supposed to be just as extinct as the Anatolian leopard.

Ian turned to look out the window next to him, where the sun was painting the clouds gold and orange.

"You know, it's funny," he said. "I was on the phone with Nellie when the others were off getting their snacks and I saw you coming out the door to the runway. But I didn't spot any of Pierce's men."

Amy could feel Ian staring at her, waiting for a response. When he didn't get one he looked up the aisle, making sure the others were absorbed in their games. He leaned in close, and when he spoke again, his voice was low and halting, as if he were picking his way through a minefield.

"Due to recent . . . events," he said, struggling with how to refer to the death of his younger sister, Natalie, "I, too, have been sometimes tempted to isolate myself but, to my surprise, I've found that having people around, even" — he glanced at the others on the plane — "*these* people, somewhat alleviates —"

"Pierce's men were there," Amy said through gritted teeth. "I'm not lying."

"I would never suggest you were," Ian said. "I simply —"

"Amy?"

The anxious roil in Amy's stomach jumped twofold when she saw Jake standing in the aisle in front of her.

"You okay?" he asked.

"We were just having ourselves a bit of a chat," Ian said. "Nothing for the likes of you to worry about."

"Atticus has some ideas he wants to run past you," Jake said to Amy.

She started to get up but Ian put his hand on hers, holding her back.

"If you keep troubling Amy with every little thing—"

"Maybe you should let Amy decide what's little and what's—"

"Guys!" Amy cried.

Ian and Jake shut up instantly, as shocked to hear Amy yell as she was to do it.

"I just need a minute," she said. "Okay? Alone? Jake, I'll be with you soon."

There was a tense pause and then Jake stalked off to the front of the plane. Ian was about to say something but Amy turned away from him, and a beat later he pushed himself up out of his seat and left.

Amy closed her eyes and tried to quiet her mind, but she kept hearing the sound of her own raised voice. Was there a worse sound, Amy wondered, than your own voice, yelling at people you love? Not only that, but she could feel that newspaper sitting in the pack next to her, like an itch demanding to be scratched. Amy pulled it out and spread it across her lap.

The headline read: THE CAHILL WEB OF EVIL.

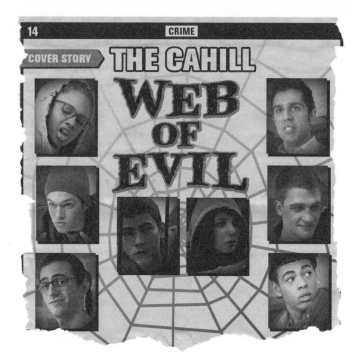

CRIME

COVER STORY THE CAHILL WEB OF EVIL

To each side, two columns of three pictures each were laid out like mug shots. Atticus, Jake, and Pony on one side and Ian, Hamilton, and Jonah on the other. Pictures of Amy and Dan — deeply shadowed in Photoshop to make them look especially sinister — sat between the columns, with spidery lines running from their pictures to the other six.

The article that accompanied the pictures alleged that Amy and Dan were not simply international nuisances, but were heading up a far-reaching criminal conspiracy with the others.

Hamilton Holt! the article screamed next to Hamilton's picture. *A burly brute who uses his fists to lay down the law on whoever dares to contradict the Cahill cabal!*

Atticus Rosenbloom — the cabal's twisted mastermind. This pint-sized provocateur uses his big brain and his connections to the worldwide academic elite to subvert the will of decent freedom-loving people everywhere!

It went on and on. Ian was a member of the global elite who provided them with an entrance into high society, while Jonah Wizard gleefully poisoned the youth of the world through insidious messages in his music. Amy could hardly breathe looking at all of it. It was one thing for Pierce to attack her and Dan, but it was something else entirely to go after their friends.

Amy looked up the aisle. Jonah was showing Hamilton a new video game while Atticus and Dan were practicing their aim by throwing Skittles into each other's mouths.

It was amazing that they could seem so normal after all they had been through. Atticus and Jake had both lost their mothers, Ian had lost his sister, and Jonah's cousin Phoenix had nearly died.

Amy crumbled the newspaper in her fist. *They've all been through so much,* she thought. *It's up to me to make sure they don't lose anything else.*

CHAPTER 3

Delaware. Trilon Pharmaceuticals.

Every square inch of Nellie Gomez's body itched.

She tried to be as subtle as she could, but it was driving her crazy. She rubbed her calves together and ground her spine into the back of her chair, but the itch didn't stop. Nellie figured it was the result of a ripped-jeans-and-Bikini-Kill-T-shirt kind of gal being forced to wear a suit made of itchy, stuffy wool; a polyester blouse; and stockings made out of some kind of unholy blend of rayon and, she was pretty sure, steel wool.

And her hair! The greatest insult of all was being forced to stand over a sink and wash out all her beautiful goth black and replace it with . . . brown! Mouse brown. Boring, boring brown.

Get over yourself, Gomez, she told herself. *If it takes a suit to find out what Pierce is doing here and stop it, then a suit it is. And if I can find Sammy while I'm here, all the better.*

Nellie opened the folder on her lap and went over the résumé she had made the night before. Looking at the crisp layout and razor-sharp bullet points, Nellie was pretty sure that even she would hire her. And *she* knew that every job description and reference on the thing was faked. Even the name she used was fake.

"Ms., uh, Gormey?"

Nellie shot out of her chair to face a slight man with a black comb-over standing in the doorway of the office.

"It is I! I mean, it's me! I mean . . ." Nellie sucked in a deep breath through her ringless nose and handed him her résumé. "I'm Nadine Gormey. That's me. I'm here for the interview."

The man motioned for Nellie to sit, then came around and deposited himself across the desk from her. While he went over her résumé, Nellie reached one painted fingernail underneath her sleeve and scratched her now reddened wrist.

"I need to be clear that the position we're looking to fill is quite junior," Comb-over said.

"That's fine!"

"But someone with your qualifications," he said, marveling at her résumé. "I mean, to have run an entire lab at Harvard while still an undergrad!"

"Yes, but I think it's always important to stay practiced in the fundamentals, you know? Like" — Nellie slipped a cheat sheet out of her pocket and into her lap — "how to perform a recrystallization or calculate a solution dilution."

"Well, I doubt you'd be called on to do anything that basic, but I applaud your sentiment. Honestly, Ms. Gormey, this is one of the most impressive résumés I've seen in quite a long time. But" — he leaned over across the desk in a kind of apology — "I would be remiss if I didn't at least call one of your references."

Nellie's heart thumped. She knew this was a possibility, but had hoped it wouldn't come up.

"Of course," Nellie said through gritted teeth. "I understand completely."

Nellie crossed her fingers as the man chose a number and dialed. *Make this work and I'll never speed again! I'll never drive the wrong way on one-way streets. Or on sidewalks!*

"What do you want?" A British voice exploded from the speaker phone. "Hurry, please, I'm on my way to catch a flight."

Nellie had never been so happy to hear Ian Kabra's snooty, infuriatingly entitled voice.

"Uh, yes, Dr., um, Kabra. This is George Takahashi from Tri—"

"Get to the point! This is about Gormey, I assume. Nadine Gormey? Have you hired her yet?"

"Well, no, I was just wondering if—"

"What in the blazes is wrong with you, man!" The speakerphone shook as Ian shouted.

You're a genius, Nellie thought. *I take back every bad thought I've ever had about you.*

"In the entire time I spent slumming at the Harvard chemistry labs," Ian continued, "Nadine Gormey was, without doubt, the only certifiable genius I ever encountered. Only a complete moron would be so stupid as to not hire her the second she walked into his office. Are you a complete moron?"

"No! I just thought—"

"Well, stop thinking, Jim!"

"It's George actually. You see I—"

"And get down on your knees right now and beg—BEG!—Nadine Gormey to take over that rattrap of an operation you're running! Beg her and just perhaps she'll deign to bring the light of reason and scientific rigor to that pit of mediocrity you call a lab. Good day, sir!"

"Well . . ."

"I said good day, sir!"

The line went dead. George was a pale sweaty mess. Even his mustache was trembling. He got ahold of himself and looked up at Nellie slowly.

"So . . . when can you start?"

Somewhere over the Mediterranean

"There it is," Atticus said from the seat next to Dan. "Your future."

A jumble of brightly colored brochures littered Dan's lap. He lifted one off the pile and held it up. Was Atticus right? Was this his future?

"You think?" Dan asked. "It doesn't seem a little . . . ridiculous?"

"Oh, man, it's so completely ridiculous." Atticus took the brochure from Dan. The jet's reading light illuminated a line of jugglers, sword swallowers, and baggy-pantsed clowns. "'Bartleby's World-Famous Clown Academy.' Were more awesome words ever written? How could you not want to do this?"

Dan and Atticus had spent the previous night brainstorming Dan's post-Cahill life over endless rounds of ice cream and Italian sodas. It seemed like a joke at first, but now, looking down at all the brochures they had printed out at the hotel, it felt incredibly real. Dan's heart raced as he sifted through them.

Each one set off a volley of fireworks in his head.

"I don't know," Dan said. "If I did the American School in Rome, we could hang out, like, every day. And then there's baseball camp. And astronaut camp! I could totally go to astronaut camp."

"You could do them all!" Atticus said, his eyes round with excitement. "It's a perk of being one of the richest thirteen-year-olds on the planet. You can do anything you want."

There was a *ding* and then the captain came over the loudspeaker announcing their descent into Tunis. Dan folded up the brochures and stuffed them in his backpack. Even with the zipper closed, Dan could feel them in there, the sheer possibility of them drumming against the fabric. He pushed the pack under the seat in front of him and turned to look down the aisle.

Amy was by herself in the last row, head down over Olivia's notebook. Except for a quick conference with the pilot, that's where she had been the entire flight. Nothing weird about her studying, of course. It was just weird that she was doing it alone. Surely she could have used Atticus's brain or his own photographic memory. Dan couldn't help but feel uneasy. Amy had been spending so much time alone ever since Turkey.

No, he corrected himself. *Ever since Evan.*

Amy's first boyfriend, Evan Tolliver, had died on a Cahill mission months ago, and ever since, Amy had spent more and more time by herself, training and studying with an intensity that almost frightened Dan.

Dan, and just about everyone else in the world, thought that whatever had been starting between her and Jake might be good for her, but for some reason, whenever the two of them were in the same room, it all just devolved into the kind of bickering Dan had done with his fifth-grade crush. Who knew. Maybe that's where Amy and Jake were headed—pulling hair and knocking ice-cream cones out of each other's hands.

Not that Dan was helping any with Amy's stress. Dan had just announced that after they stopped Pierce, he was leaving the Cahill family. Leaving her. Maybe Amy was the one who needed a relaxing month or two at Bartleby's Clown Academy.

As soon as the plane bumped to a landing and slid into its private gate, Dan jumped up.

"Okay, everybody!" he announced. "Welcome to beautiful downtown Tunis! The local temperature is hot with a slight chance of incredibly, ridiculously hot. Here's the plan! Atticus and Jake, you two go talk to your dad and see what you can find out about the silphium. Amy and I will hit the Carthage ruins and see what we can find there. Ian and Hamilton, we need a hotel and possibly a local guide."

"I'm certain I can find something at least minimally acceptable," Ian said.

"Good. And while you're out there, don't forget to make fun of the locals for their fashion sense. They love that. Now, Jonah and Pony—"

"Dan, wait!"

Everyone's head turned to the back of the plane, where Amy was standing with her backpack slung over her shoulder.

"Change of plans," she said. "Except for Dan and me, everyone is heading back to Attleboro."

Jake stood up in his seat. "What? Why?"

Amy held up her hand to silence everyone. "The only way we're going to find everything we need for the antidote in time is if we break up into teams."

Amy held up several bundles of paper with her handwriting all over them.

"I've copied Olivia's notebook into separate packs," she said. "We'll have three research teams and one retrieval team. Each research team will be responsible for one of the ingredients. Anything you learn is funneled to Dan and me, and we'll retrieve it. Jonah and Hamilton, you'll be team Tikal. Ian and Pony are on Angkor duty. Jake and Atticus, you're going to stay on silphium."

"Which we can do best here," Jake said. "Seeing as how this is where the stuff, you know, *is*."

"Exactly!" Dan interjected. "And besides, Amy, you and I can't go talk to Dr. Rosenbloom. The last time he saw us, he called Interpol. He hates us. Right, Att?"

"No!" Atticus said. "Of course not. My dad just . . ."

Dan looked to his friend with one eyebrow raised.

Atticus flushed. "Okay, fine. He does. Like a lot."

"Atticus and Jake can talk to him on the phone and report back to us," Amy said.

"Now wait a minute," Jake said. "You may be the

leader of the Cahills. But, as you're so fond of reminding us, Atticus and I are *not* Cahills. So if you think you can stop us from staying in Tunis and seeing our own father, you're crazy."

"I'm not trying to stop you from seeing your father," Amy said. "I'm just trying to get the job done."

"Guys, guys, guys," Dan said, forcing himself in between Amy and Jake. "You're going to give our new friend Pony the wrong idea about us. He doesn't know that while we argue occasionally, we all share a deep love and abiding respect that rises above petty little quarrels."

"This isn't *little*," Jake said. "She doesn't have the right to do this."

"No," Amy said. "*He* doesn't have the right to—"

"Hey!" Dan said, pushing the two of them apart. "You know what we need? Pizza! Or the local equivalent. We'll have a bite and then we'll sit down and we'll *all* make a plan together."

Amy shoved past Dan and Jake to the plane's exit. "We don't have time to stand around talking," she said. "The plan is made."

"Amy, wait!" Dan called, but she was already gone.

Everyone left in the plane turned and silently stared at Dan. He backed delicately toward the plane's exit, his best fake smile plastered across his face.

"Don't worry, guys," he said. "This is a minor hiccup caused by, uh, extreme jet lag. Why don't you guys just hang out here on the plane. I'll be right back!"

Dan dashed out of the plane before anyone could

say a word. He found his sister striding through the intense afternoon sun toward their gate.

"Amy! Hey, Amy. Wait up!" Dan called, jogging to catch up to her. "What was that all about?"

"This isn't pee-wee soccer," Amy said without missing a step. "We don't have time to make sure everybody is playing the position they want. We have work to do."

"Which we do best when we're all together. Seriously, Amy, I don't think—"

Amy whipped something out of her backpack and pushed it into Dan's chest. A newspaper.

"What's this?"

Amy said nothing. Dan took the paper and opened it. His eyes went wide as he turned from page to page.

"But this . . . none of this is true," he sputtered. "He can't just—"

"He can," Amy said. "Anybody standing with us is a target, Dan, and Pierce is not playing around anymore. The FBI is already looking at us back home. What if Pierce's stories convince them to start going after the others, too? Think about Jonah's music career. Or how Atticus wants to go to Harvard. You and I *have* to be here, Dan, none of them do."

"Just because they're back home doesn't mean they'll be safe."

"No, but they'll be safer," Amy said. "It's the best we can do."

Something inside of Dan sank painfully. The paper dangled in his hands.

"Jake and Att have to stay," he said.

Amy started to say something, but Dan cut her off. "We can't waste time sending them all the way home just to talk to their dad on the phone. The only way we're getting this done in time is if they're here."

There was a roar behind them as another plane lifted off into the skies above Tunis.

"Fine," Amy said. "But as soon as we're done here, they both go back to Attleboro. No arguments. Agreed?"

Dan met his sister's green eyes. For the first time, they resembled stone. "Agreed."

Amy watched as Dan stood by the plane, fending off angry questions from Hamilton and Ian. He must have been convincing, since he managed to talk them all back inside. Dan went up the stairs to help Jake and Atticus with their things, leaving Ian alone at the back of the line.

Amy's heart ached as Ian looked at her across the runway. He was a Kabra, so his hurt was concealed beneath a veil of pride, but Amy could see it as plain as the desert sun burning over her head. She knew she was doing this for Ian's own good, but she also knew how much their mission distracted him from what he had lost. Maybe one day he'd understand.

Amy turned away, fixing her eyes on the terminal and heading for it.

"Amy! Wait!"

She turned back to see Pony rushing up toward her.

"Sorry!" Pony said when he reached her, huffing and puffing. "Almost forgot!" He pulled a small padded envelope out of his pocket and held it out to her. "Some mail came after you left Attleboro. Wanted to bring it to you."

"Thanks."

Pony ran back to the jet, saying good-bye to Jake and Atticus as Dan led them out of the plane. Amy turned the package over. Her name and address were on the front, but there was no return. She tore it open and pulled out a single sheet of paper.

Amy,

Sorry again for messing things up with the serum. Took a look around the lab and figured out how to make one more dose. Thought you might need it.

Sammy Mourad

Amy dug back into the envelope, heart racing. She found something inside and pulled it out. It was a small glass vial, half filled with serum.

"Hey, Amy, whatcha got there?" asked Dan.

Amy dropped the vial back into the envelope and stuffed it into her backpack.

"Nothing," she said. "Nothing at all."

Tunis, Tunisia

Less than an hour later, they had found themselves a hotel and Atticus was leading the group through Tunis on Avenue Habib Bourguiba. Amy had to admit that Ian was right. The avenue was nothing if not fashionable. She didn't see any discos, but she did see smart-looking shoppers darting in and out of boutiques or lounging in the sidewalk cafés. The street itself was lined with well-manicured ficus trees and ornate black streetlights. All of it sat beneath a shockingly blue sky.

"Att," Jake said. "You're sure Dad's library is this way?"

"Yep. Past here and into the medina."

"The medina?" Dan asked.

"It's like the old part of the city," Atticus said. "Well, the old part of the city that still stands. There's been a major city on this site for nearly three thousand years. The *really* old part of the city is the ruins of Punic Carthage to the north."

"Puny Carthage?" Dan asked. "Like, little tiny wimpy Carthage?"

"No," Atticus said. "Punic like Phoenician. See. Okay. We don't know much for sure about Carthage, but we think it might have been founded by a Phoenician queen named Elissa. Only, when Virgil wrote about her in the *Aeneid*, he decided to call her Queen Dido instead. Anyway, what we know about her is kind of a mix of legend and possibly fact."

"That's pretty confidence inspiring, Atticus," Dan said.

"Give me a break! We're talking like three thousand years of history here. Anyway, the legend and *maybe* sorta kinda fact is that Elissa and her brother Pygmalion were supposed to share the throne of Phoenicia when their father died. But! Pygmalion killed their father and then killed Elissa's husband. Not being suicidal, I guess, Elissa took a bunch of her people and got as far away from her brother as she could."

"Apparently," Jake said, "the locals weren't too thrilled to have her and her people here, so she told the local king she only wanted as much land as could be encompassed by a single ox hide. When he said okay, she tore the ox hide into tiny little strips and surrounded an entire hill with it. Totally conned the guy."

"*Or,*" Amy said, "she did what she had to do to protect herself and her people."

"Right," Jake said. "The end totally justifies the means."

"I didn't say that!"

"So," Dan cut in as he wedged himself in between Amy and Jake, sending them to opposite sides of the sidewalk. "If Carthage was such a big deal, then why do we know so little about it?"

"Because," Jake said, "Rome completely wiped them out after the Third Punic War."

"Then, after the Romans," Atticus said, "this place was conquered again by the Vandals—no, not that kind of vandal, Dan. They were a Germanic tribe that conquered a lot of North Africa and the Mediterranean—and then the Byzantines and then the Arabs. Then the French took over, and now they're on their own."

"Man, everybody wanted a piece of Carthage."

"It was a pretty good strategic location and the farming was amazing, apparently. When Rome was in charge, they called the place the granary of the empire."

"Did they grow any silphium?" Amy asked.

Atticus shrugged.

"Olivia seemed to think so," Dan said.

"All we know is she thinks silphium had some *connection* to Carthage," Atticus said. "What that is, is anyone's guess. Leonardo da Vinci suggested she look for it on the 'Island of the Athenian,' but since Athens was the capital of Greece and *not* an island, Olivia figured it was his idea of a joke."

"Hilarious," Dan said.

"So what is silphium, exactly?" Amy asked.

"Some kind of plant," Jake said. "We don't even know for sure what it looked like, since it's been extinct for something like a thousand years."

Amy shook her head. "If we don't know what it looked like, how can we be sure it's extinct? I mean, there could be groves of the stuff and we wouldn't know."

They had moved from the ficus-lined Habib Bourguiba to a broad plaza of what looked like white marble crisscrossed by sharp geometric patterns. Towering in front of them was a great stone edifice with an arched tunnel cutting straight through it.

"Bab el Bahr!" Atticus marveled. "The entire medina used to be surrounded by a stone wall. The wall is gone now but these portals still remain."

The plaza was packed with people moving in every direction. A babel of conversations in French and Arabic mixed with the splash of a fountain and the shouts of the sellers standing at umbrella-covered stalls.

Amy held her breath as they started down the road into the medina. It was incredibly narrow, hemmed in by lines of merchants' stalls stacked up against the two- or three-story buildings on either side. The kiosks were teeming with goods, laid out on tables and hanging from the roofs of the stalls. Everywhere the kids looked, there were glittering stacks of brass and tin, along with elegantly shaped ceramics and bolts of fabrics in brilliant reds and greens and lapis blue. Dark alleyways and winding arteries shot off the main road in a confusion of directions.

When Amy turned to Dan, she saw he was doing the same thing she was. Scanning rooftops and open windows, examining the faces of the sellers that seemed to be everywhere. It was second nature to them now, to look for an ambush.

Something caught Amy's eye and she veered off the street to a merchant's kiosk.

"What's up?" Dan asked, moving in next to her.

"Look at these, Dan, aren't they pretty?"

Amy picked up one of the man's beaten copper pots and handed it to her brother. "One o'clock," she whispered. "By the rug merchant's stall."

Dan lifted the copper pot up into the light, then turned it like he was examining a defect. Jake and Atticus appeared behind them.

"What's going on?" Jake asked.

"Oh, nothing," Amy said to Jake just loud enough so he could hear. "We were looking at these for Nellie. You know how she loves to be *ambushed* with gifts."

Dan put the pot back. "Guy in the hat?" he asked. "Doesn't look like any of the ones we've seen."

"Who knows how many guys Pierce has," Amy whispered.

"There's another one," Atticus said. "Near the flower stall. Westerner. New to the area."

"How can you tell?"

"His face is pink," Jake said. "Sunburn."

"What do we do?" Dan asked.

"Follow him," Jake said. "See what we can learn."

Amy thought a second, then backed away from the table. "No. We go back to the hotel."

"But he could lead us right to their base," Jake whispered urgently. "We could see how many of them there are, find out their plans—"

"Get ourselves killed. No," Amy said. "We stick to the plan! Get the silphium and get out."

But Jake was already on the move. Amy reached for his sleeve but he was too fast. Jake threw himself into the river of shoppers and disappeared around a corner. Amy whirled around to find that the man in the hat was gone, too.

"Stay here!" she yelled at Dan and Atticus before diving into the crowd. Did Jake even care that he could get himself killed?

Amy struggled through the crowded medina. Despite her best efforts, she seemed to slam into shoppers at every step, earning her insults in at least three languages. She searched the chaos for a glimpse of Jake or the man with the hat, but all she saw were kiosks and bodies and twisting roads.

"There he is!" Dan called out.

Jake appeared at the other end of an alley, speeding down a street that ran parallel to their own.

"I told you two to wait!" Amy yelled over her shoulder as she took off after Jake.

Amy screamed inwardly as Dan shot past her, pounding down the alleyway that connected the two streets. Jake had disappeared again by the time they spilled into the road, but Amy caught sight of the man with the hat as he headed toward a towering mosque.

"If we take that road, we can get between him and Jake," Amy said.

Brass and iron clattered against the ground as Amy barreled past more merchants, jostling their stalls. She ignored their cries, keeping her eye on the man as he slipped expertly through the crowds. When they were just feet from the plaza, the man turned down a stone-roofed alley. Half a second later, Jake emerged from the crowds and followed him in.

Amy, Dan, and Atticus stopped at the mouth of the alley, panting. Amy peered down its length. It was long and even narrower than the streets. The harsh sun only managed to light the first few feet, and beyond was a murk so dark it looked like night. Somewhere down there, Jake was alone with a monster.

Amy looked back at Dan wheezing behind her. He nodded and they both began to move. Atticus started to join them but Amy held him back.

"We need a lookout," she whispered.

"But—"

Amy raised a finger to her lips to silence Atticus and then followed Dan into the alley. It was even darker than she imagined and full of the vinegary smell of moldering trash. The sounds of the city and the markets were muted by the alley's walls, filling the tunnel with a whispering hush. Amy crept forward, her body on high alert. Dan had slipped farther ahead and was lost in the shadows. Amy felt panic building up in her. Then a single shaft of sunlight from a gap in the stone roof fell some thirty feet ahead. There was a flash of white as the man in the hat stepped into it.

"Amy Cahill," the man said. His voice was pleasant, but had a flinty British accent. "And Dan and Jake. I believe that's Atticus Rosenbloom watching the alley. Am I right?"

Amy found a loose paving stone at her feet. She grabbed it and held it at the ready. "What do you want?"

"To talk."

"About what?"

The man turned toward her, one hand reaching inside his jacket.

"He's got a gun!" Jake cried as he exploded out of the gloom only feet from Amy. The man was ready for him, though. He pivoted toward Jake, but Amy leaped up and shoved Jake into the brick wall, putting herself between him and the British mercenary.

"Amy! Jake!"

It was Atticus. A tide of bodies was pushing past him and into the alley. More of Pierce's goons. It was a trap! Amy turned back to the man in the hat just as Dan slammed into him from behind.

"Dan!"

There was nothing to do now but fight. The man stumbled at Dan's strike, but managed to push him aside so Dan went reeling farther into the alley. It was the perfect distraction. Jake appeared by Amy's side and together they took the man by the shoulders and flung him around and into the wall. He hit the brick with a satisfying *oof*, and Jake swung for him. There was a crack as he connected with the man's chin, sending him slumping into the dirt.

Jake looked back at Amy, but they barely had a second to relax before a blast of white light filled the alley. Amy staggered back, shielding her eyes. There was another flash, and another. This time from the man on the ground. His hand had emerged from his jacket and he was holding some sort of a device. Not a gun but . . .

"Smile, kids!"

Everything snapped into focus. Not a gun. A camera. A flash went off and Amy turned toward the charging mass of people to face a firing squad of flashes. Everyone was shouting. A slight woman in a tan suit pushed a microphone in her face.

"Amy! Do you plan to brutalize any other people while in Tunis or just this innocent reporter?"

Amy's mouth fell open, stunned. The reporters surged forward, crowding the kids deeper into the alley. Dan picked himself up and joined Amy and Jake. The man in the hat got up, camera in hand. There was blood running down his chin, but he was smiling.

"Hey, Jake! How does it feel to join a global criminal conspiracy?"

"Was it hard to bring your innocent little brother into it, too?"

"Dan! Will you ever be able to wipe your nose without your big sister's okay?"

"Leave us alone!" Amy shouted, and ran at them, driving her way through the crowd, which had become as thick as a forest. Hands reached out to her from every direction as the reporters pushed their business cards into her pockets.

"Call me, Amy!"

"How does it feel to be personally responsible for the death of Evan Tolliver?"

Amy spun toward the reporter, her hand curling into a fist. But Jake appeared on one side of her and Dan on the other. They dragged her back through the crowds as the reporters took picture after picture. Atticus was waiting at the head of the alley with a cab idling behind him, its back doors thrown open.

Jake and Dan tossed Amy into the cab and then jumped in behind her. Atticus hopped into the front seat and slammed the door.

"Go!" Atticus shouted. "Now!"

"Unbelievable," Jake said, cradling his bruised hand. "They're worse than Pierce's goons."

Amy glared at Jake across the backseat of the taxi.

"Yeah," she said. "And you gave them exactly what they wanted."

CHAPTER 6

To make sure they evaded the reporters, Atticus had the driver lead them on a high-speed ramble through Tunis. They were on a highway, then off again. By the lake, on the Habib Bourguiba, back in the medina. A tense silence filled the cab the entire way. Amy stared out one window while Jake stared out the other. Dan squirmed between them.

"Where to now?" Dan asked Amy, breaking the quiet. "The hotel?"

"Those reporters are going to be staking out every hotel in Tunis looking for us," Amy said. "Att, have the driver take us to your dad. We might as well get something accomplished."

Minutes later, the taxi skidded to a halt outside the gates of an ornate building. The three of them tumbled out of the backseat of the car as Atticus paid the driver. Once Jake introduced himself to the guard just inside the library, they were all given badges and shown through a set of double doors.

"Can I see Olivia's notebook again?" Atticus asked.

Amy dug in her bag and handed it over. It was amazing to watch him, she thought. Ninety percent of the time, Atticus looked like any other twelve-year-old on the street, but not when he read. He seemed older than *her* then. He lost himself in it, his forehead furrowing into thin ridges and his eyes going sharp as cut glass. She had the decoded notes in her bag, but it was like Atticus didn't even need them. Once he had broken the code, he could read right through it.

Jake was watching his brother, too, clearly just as amazed as she was. When Jake felt Amy watching him, he turned toward her, his face brightening in a smile. Amy felt a jolt of nerves and turned away from him, continuing on down the hall.

Small offices lined the hall on either side, each one filled with enough scientists in tweed and lab coats to fill a university. All of them were bent over ancient rocks and scrolls of paper. Even their murmurs sounded smart.

"Wow," Dan said. "This place is nerd central. Amy, we have *got* to get you a job here."

They came to the end of the hallway and an office with *Dr. Rosenbloom* on the doorplate.

"Okay," Jake said. "You two wait out here while Atticus and I see what we can learn."

Jake was about to close the door behind them but Amy shoved her hand between the door and the jamb. She hissed with pain but managed to keep it open a crack without attracting Jake's attention.

Dr. Rosenbloom's office reminded Amy of a library that had been struck by a tornado. Books and journals and newspapers covered every square inch of the place, most of them underlined and highlighted and powdered with dust. Old dishes and tea-stained mugs were stacked in listing towers beside walls of half-opened mail. The place didn't seem dirty, exactly, it just seemed like the space of a man with a million thoughts going through his head at once.

The only part of the office that was at all well-ordered were the shelves stuffed with books relating to Dr. Rosenbloom's singular obsession — ancient or lost civilizations. Amy was stunned by the sheer number and variety of them. Books on the Ancestral Pueblo People and the Minoans and the Olmecs sat beside ones on more fanciful lost civilizations like El Dorado. Two whole shelves were filled with nothing but books on Atlantis.

We've definitely come to the right place, Amy thought.

"Atticus! Jakey!" Dr. Rosenbloom appeared at the office's back door, beaming. He threw his arms open and gathered his sons into his chest, glowing with joy. Amy had to admit that Dr. Rosenbloom was quite something. He was a perfect mixture of Jake and Atticus. He had the broad shoulders and square jaw of an athlete but the unkempt clothes and the thick-rimmed glasses of a globe-trotting slob/genius.

The best thing of all was how much he clearly loved his sons. Amy felt a twinge deep in her chest.

She looked at Dan and guessed from the dark, focused look on his face as he watched them that he was feeling the same thing. A real parent. Something they'd had for such a short time.

Dr. Rosenbloom swept stacks of books and papers off the chairs in his office and sat the boys down. He had two paper sacks in hand and set them on his desk.

"Okay! First things first, I grabbed us some lunch. Tajine malsouka! This is going to blow your minds, guys. It's like a chicken pie made with phyllo dough. My friend Amina makes it."

Jake and Atticus shared an amused look. Their dad *always* had a woman friend who was making him things to eat. Dr. Rosenbloom opened the bag and pulled out what looked like thick pieces of pie wrapped in waxed paper. The office filled with the smells of spicy chicken and warm bread. Amy had to grab on to Dan's shoulder to keep him from busting through the door and into the room.

"So tell me everything!" Dr. Rosenbloom said through a mouthful of pie. "How's school?"

"Good!" Atticus said, maybe a little too quickly. "The independent study is going really well."

"Awesome," Dr. Rosenbloom said. "Harvard won't know what hit them when you get there. What brings you guys from Rome, though? I'm happy you came, of course, but it's such short notice. Is everything all right?"

"Fine!" Jake said. "We just wanted to see you. And

Atticus had some questions. About his independent study."

"Happy to help. What is it?"

"Well, I'm looking at agriculture," Atticus said. "Particularly the major Roman crops and who produced them outside of Italy."

"*Fascinating* topic."

Dan rolled his eyes and Amy elbowed him hard in the side.

"It is," Atticus continued. "But I keep coming across one crop that I can't find much about. Silphium."

Dr. Rosenbloom nodded eagerly, swallowing a mouthful. "Mmm. Well, that's probably because there's not much anyone can say. It was one of the biggest and most sought after crops of its time, which was about the seventh century B.C. to the first century A.D. The Romans said it was worth its weight in silver."

"So what did it do?" Jake asked.

Dr. Rosenbloom laughed. "Everything, apparently. People used it as a seasoning in their food and as a general-purpose remedy. Cured just about anything you could name. Or so they said. Here, guys, have some more."

Dr. Rosenbloom loaded Jake and Atticus up with fresh slices of pie.

"Well, if it was so great, how did it go extinct?" Jake asked. "Why didn't people just grow more?"

"No one really knows," Dr. Rosenbloom said, leaning back and brushing crumbs off of his rumpled tie.

"Maybe they went through it too fast and then there was a crop failure. Some people said it only grew wild and couldn't be cultivated, but that seems unlikely."

"Was it grown here in Carthage?"

"Carthage?" Dr. Rosenbloom asked. "No, the main grower was Cyrene if I remember correctly. That's Libya today. It's close by but I don't remember reading anything about it being grown here. Why?"

"Just part of the project," Atticus said quickly. "Kind of like a scavenger hunt. We're supposed to try and find some, and my adviser thought we could try here."

"A scavenger hunt? For something that doesn't exist? Atticus, that's a total waste of your time. Who's your adviser? I should call and straighten him out."

Dr. Rosenbloom reached back to a phone on his desk.

"No!" Atticus said. "It's fine. Really." Atticus jumped up to stop his dad, and when he did Olivia's notebook fell out of his hand and onto the table.

"What's this?"

"Nothing! It's just—"

Amy suppressed a gasp as Dr. Rosenbloom took the notebook off the table and opened it.

"Really," Jake said. "It's not anything. Just—"

Jake stopped. An almost physical transformation came over Dr. Rosenbloom as he read. His soft and bright features turned a hard, ashy gray. Amy started forward, but Dan held her back.

"I thought you said you came because you wanted

to see me," Dr. Rosenbloom said with a dark frown.

"Dad . . ." Jake started.

"Olivia CAHILL!?" he shouted, brandishing the notebook in their faces. "I told you I didn't want you getting involved with the Cahills ever again."

"We're not. We're just—"

"Don't lie to me, Jake!"

Dr. Rosenbloom's shout echoed in the small office.

"We told them we'd see what we could find out about the silphium," Atticus said. "That's all."

"You've seen the stories about them in the papers," Dr. Rosenbloom said. "On TV. Is that what you want to be a part of? You want to be famous?"

"Those stories aren't true!" Atticus protested.

"Think about your future, Atticus. And Jake's. I know you think Amy and Dan are your friends, but if they were, they wouldn't let you get involved in these things." He held up the notebook between them. "The Cahills don't care about anybody but themselves and their stupid games, and they never have!"

Amy fell back from the door, squeezing her eyes shut as if she could block it out, but his words were like knives tearing into her. There was a thump as Dr. Rosenbloom threw Olivia's notebook onto the tabletop.

"They're not games," Jake cried. "This is important, and Amy and Dan—"

Jake suddenly went quiet, and Amy looked back into the room. Olivia's notebook was lying open on the desk and Dr. Rosenbloom was leaning over it, completely absorbed in something inside that had caught his eye. Dr. Rosenbloom drew the book off the counter and into his lap, flipping quickly through the pages.

"Dad?" Atticus said.

Dr. Rosenbloom held up one hand and turned another page. The lines of hurt fell away and his face took on the same diamond-like focus that Atticus had when he was reading.

"Not possible," Dr. Rosenbloom muttered to himself, shaking his head. "It's not possible."

"What isn't possible?" Jake asked. "Dad!"

"It was right under my nose the whole time!"

Jake reached across the desk and shook his father's arm, forcing him to emerge from the book. Dr. Rosenbloom snapped it shut. "I want you two on a plane back to Rome."

Jake started to protest but Dr. Rosenbloom shut him down. "No discussion. You two leave tonight, and call me as soon as you get in."

"But what did you read?" Jake asked as his father tore through the room, filling a messy briefcase with papers and stacks of books from his shelves.

"Tonight, Jake!"

Dr. Rosenbloom threw on a jacket and headed toward the door. Amy and Dan jumped forward, hiding behind the door as Dr. Rosenbloom threw it open and hit the hall at a run. His footsteps clattered down the hallway past his astonished coworkers. Papers flew out of his half-closed briefcase. A door at the end of the hall flew open and he was gone.

Jake and Atticus joined Dan and Amy in the now silent hallway.

"Uh . . . guys?" Dan said. "What the heck was that?"

"No idea," Atticus said, visibly shaken. "I've never seen him get like that before."

"You three better go back to the hotel," Amy said. "Dig into the notebook and figure out what he saw. It *has* to be important."

"What are you going to do?" Dan asked.

"Head to the Carthage ruins. There's a museum there, too. Maybe I can learn some more."

"I'll go with you," Jake said.

"No," Amy said quickly, already rushing down the hall. "You stay here and help the others."

"But, Amy—"

Amy threw open the double doors, stumbling into the bright heat of Tunis. She made it around the side of the building and out of sight before collapsing with her back against a wall. She was surprised to find her breath coming fast and her heart pounding. Dr. Rosenbloom's words echoed in her head. *The Cahills don't care about anybody but themselves.*

Behind her, the doors to the library opened and voices filled the courtyard. Dan and Jake and Atticus. Amy pushed herself away from the wall and disappeared down the streets of Tunis.

CHAPTER 7

Cara Pierce stepped into the dojo as the clock struck noon. Her brother, Galt, stood across from her, barefoot in his black uniform and black belt. He snapped into a fighting stance with a snarl.

The dojo was spacious, with clean white walls and a polished floor of blond wood. A weapons rack holding bamboo swords, staffs, and nunchakus sat along one wall. Up in a high corner, a single black video camera swiveled back and forth. Cara knew her father was at his desk, watching on a monitor. When they were done, he would descend and give the winner a reward.

When they were kids, the reward for Galt and Cara's weekly sparring matches was ice cream or a new toy, but as they got older the winner received an extra helping of their father's most prized, most hoarded possession — his time. The winner sat in his meetings, listened to his plans, helped him conspire. The loser was shut out.

Of course, sometimes Cara wasn't sure what she

wanted more — her father's favor or to wipe the vicious smirk off of her brother's face.

Cara dropped into her own stance, but before she could make a move there was a blur of movement followed by a crunching impact to her jaw. The world flipped and Cara found herself on her back. She cursed herself for her distraction and leaped back to her feet. She managed a quick roundhouse kick that connected with Galt's side but he flashed away.

Galt had always been fast and strong, but in the last few weeks, he seemed to border on inhuman. One minute he was safely on her left, and then without warning he was on her right, sending a punch flying toward her temple. Cara got a few punches in but they came more and more infrequently while Galt bounced back from them faster every time.

Always, out of the corner of her eye, she could see that black camera tracking them.

Cara spun away from another crushing blow. Along with her father's favors came the lectures. Survival of the fittest is what he always said. Winners rose to the top through hard work and God-given talent. And losers? All they were good for was doing the bidding of the winners.

Cara had an idea. Instead of circling away from Galt as their sensei had taught, she slid straight back from him, dodging a flurry of blows. Galt growled as he came at her, working himself into a frenzy, his eyes ablaze.

That's right, Cara thought. *Keep coming. You may be strong and fast, but it's time to see which one of us is smart.*

Cara slowed and let him land a right on her side. It was like taking a freight train in the ribs. Cara stifled a scream and responded with a worthless punch and then a side kick that went nowhere. Galt laughed and landed a stunning combination. Right left right. Straight kick. Roundhouse. Cara's breath left her in a rush and she went down in a heap.

Galt stood before her, hands on his hips, self-satisfied grin flashing. Cara crawled over to the weapons rack and grabbed the top rail. She slowly pulled herself up, finally making it to her knees and draping her arms over the lip of the wooden rack. She didn't have to fake it now. Every inch of her body throbbed with pain.

Galt sauntered over, reveling in the opportunity to mock her. "Need some help there, sis?"

Cara looked over her shoulder. The black surveillance camera in the corner was right on them. Galt was holding out his hand, cocky smile burning. Cara smiled right back.

"Nope."

Cara swept a bamboo sword out of the rack and swung with all her might. Galt's eyes went wide as the shaft whistled through the air.

"Hey! This isn't a weapons drill! Cara!"

Cara laughed as her brother retreated, varying her strikes to keep him off balance. She went right, then left, a hard jab to the stomach with the sword point to knock the wind out of him, and then a spinning kick to his side. Galt went down with a cry and Cara stood over him, triumphant, her bare foot on his stomach, the sword at his throat.

"Okay!" Galt cried. "You win! I surrender!"

"You get overconfident, bro," Cara said with a smile of her own. "Get to thinking you're invincible when you're not."

"Funny," Galt said. "I was just thinking the same thing about you."

"What do you—?"

Before Cara could react, the sword was out of her hands and in Galt's. And he was back on his feet. *How did he—?* Galt whirled the sword like a helicopter blade, gaining momentum before slamming it into Cara's side, and shoulder, and back. Each strike was perfectly aimed, hitting a jutting bone or a nerve point. Cara feinted left and then moved right, but the bamboo blade came out of nowhere, sending her crashing into the wooden rack.

When she managed to look up, Galt was striding toward her, grinning.

"Sorry, sis," he said with a shrug. "I guess there's just no fighting God-given talent."

Cara shut her eyes and Galt lifted the sword, tensing up for the blow.

"Enough!"

Their father stood in the doorway. He looked like a marble statue in his inky-black suit.

"Dad!" Galt said. "Did you see? I totally beat Cara!"

"But, Dad," Cara cried as she struggled to get to her feet. "He surrendered!"

"I did not!"

"You did! Dad, Galt totally—"

"What? Cheated?" her father replied acidly. "Only losers whine about rules, Cara. Rules and regulations were put in place to coddle the weak, and Pierces are not weak! Now, I believe your mother could use some help arranging her teddy bear collection. Of course, if you don't want this to happen again, maybe you should hit the gym more often."

"Yes, sir."

"Galt," he said as he stepped into the hallway outside. "You're with me."

As soon as their father's back was turned, Galt stuck his tongue out at Cara and then slipped out into the hall. The door slammed behind them, and Cara forced herself to her feet and started lurching toward the gym. She'd show Dad and Galt, too. She'd train harder than ever. Longer, too.

I'll show them both who's stronger.

CHAPTER 8

Amy wandered for more than an hour before she gathered the courage to admit something very important.

She was lost.

The cabdriver who picked her up in the medina spoke Arabic, French, and Italian, but no English. So the best Amy could do was repeat *Carthage, museum,* and *north* over and over again. Finally, the man waved his hand and hit the gas, driving at terrifying speeds before screeching to a halt in the middle of a small town. When she questioned him, he pointed vaguely, then sped off in a cloud of exhaust.

Amy tried to figure out where she was using her phone, but reception was almost nonexistent.

As frustrating as it was, Amy had to admit there were worse places to be lost. The town she found herself in sat on a palm tree–covered hill with a wide view of the Mediterranean below. The narrow streets were lined with low buildings, each one painted snowy white with accents of the deepest blue Amy had ever seen. Residents lounged on wide porches, soaking up the last rays of the sun, while tourists drifted down the avenue, visiting the few merchant stalls that hung on despite the gathering dark.

Amy paused at a corner and looked down on boats gliding into a small marina for the night. She was surprised to find the strain of the day begin to fade.

Is this what Dan wants? Amy wondered. The fact that her brother was leaving after they beat Pierce was never far from her mind. *To come to a place like this and simply . . . be. No running. No fighting.*

Amy couldn't imagine it. And what would he say the next time someone like Pierce turned up? "Sorry, world! Got to work on my tan."

No, Amy thought. *Dan and I are Cahills. It isn't just what we do, it's who we are. If we stopped, if we split up, what's left? Who would we even be?*

Amy pushed it out of her head. Dan's talk was just that—talk. After they finished with Pierce, she'd make sure he got some time off. Let him go sit on a beach. After a little downtime, she was sure he'd forget about it. Satisfied, Amy struck out again down the road.

"Excuse me? The Carthage Museum?" she asked.

Tourist after tourist either shook their head or pointed generally to the south. The sun was setting fast. Amy needed to move. She hiked her backpack up on her shoulders and headed down the road.

"You're looking for the Carthage Museum?" A man's voice came from behind her.

Finally! "Yes!" Amy said, turning back. "I guess I

just got a little—"

Jake Rosenbloom was leaning against one of the clean white walls, an infuriating grin plastered across his face. "Lost?"

"What are *you* doing here?"

"Looks like I'm rescuing you."

"I know exactly where I'm going!" Amy insisted, turning and pointing down the road. "It's . . . that way!"

Amy would have thought it impossible if she hadn't seen it herself. His grin actually grew wider. Jake stepped out of her way. "Well, after you, then. I've *always* wanted to see the Carthage Museum."

Amy turned and continued down the street. She winced at the sound of Jake's sneakers behind her.

"So how'd you end up here anyway?" Jake asked in an overly chipper tone. "Cabdriver not speak English?"

Amy ignored him. The street took a sharp turn and started heading downhill into thicker darkness.

"It's just funny," Jake went on. "Since if I remember correctly, you're traveling with people who have a working knowledge of Arabic and Italian. Some French, too!"

"Shouldn't you be looking after Dan and Atticus?"

"They're fine," Jake said. "Hunting the mythical Tunisian pizza. The three of us figured we'd all go back to Dad's house later on tonight and get everything sorted out. Once he's cooled down, he'll listen. Atticus thought it might actually go better if you and

Dan made a direct appeal."

"Oh, right, because he *loves* us."

"Don't worry, we're going to let Dan do the talking. His record on not infuriating people who are only trying to help is way better than yours."

Amy wanted to scream but she forced herself to keep walking. The farther they went, the darker it got. Soon, Amy began to hear the crashing of waves. Getting closer to the beach meant they were walking east, not south. Amy searched for roads branching off in that direction but saw nothing. Of course, if she turned back, she'd have to face Jake's I-told-you-so glee, so she put her head down and kept going.

We'll get to the bottom of this hill and the road will turn south, Amy told herself. *Right to the museum.*

Of course, it didn't. Several minutes later Amy found herself ankle deep in sand, just down the beach from the marina. Her frustration was nearly at a boil. At her side, Jake made a noise that sounded suspiciously like a laugh.

"Don't. Say. A. Word."

"No!" he said. "Absolutely not. I just didn't know that the Carthage Museum was one of those new invisible floating museums," Jake said, unable to control his laughter any longer. "Look, Amy, you need to just —"

"What? Relax? Oh! Yes! Why don't we all just relax?" Amy screamed. "I mean all we have on the agenda is defeating a lunatic who has hired teams of serum-enhanced assassins to kill us. Oh! And then your dad, the number one person we needed to help us, just completely freaks out! For no reason! And then the taxi driver doesn't speak English and my phone doesn't work and I CAN'T EVEN FIND A STUPID MUSEUM!!"

Jake looked up at the gaggle of tourists hanging out by the marina. "Uh . . . Amy. Maybe you should—"

"And to top it all off, my stupid brother suddenly wants to retire at thirteen *and* I have to deal with you! You, who just shows up out of nowhere with your smug attitude and your perfect hair and your big stupid face that looks like it's carved out of marble."

"You really think my hair is perfect?"

"Ahhh!"

Amy stomped away through the sand, leaving Jake and heading toward the marina.

"Amy, wait!"

"I'm going to go find a cab."

"Hey! Are you Amy Cahill?"

Two men in suits stood between Amy and the marina. One of them reached inside his jacket.

"Oh, great! And now I have to deal with you people, too. What? You want more pictures for your stupid newspaper? Well, go right ahead and take them!"

One of them laughed. "We're not here to take pictures, Ms. Cahill."

"Then what are you here for!?"

The man smiled and pulled his hand out of his jacket, but instead of a camera Amy found herself staring down the barrel of a very large gun.

CHAPTER 9

"Duck!"

Amy dropped to her knees as a cloud of sand flew over her head and into the eyes of the two men. Jake grabbed her by the shoulders and yanked her to her feet.

"Run!"

Amy and Jake took off toward the marina, right into the crowd of onlookers who had all turned toward them in varying states of shock. The men were behind them and closing the distance incredibly fast. These were definitely Pierce's thugs. Amy caught a glint of bronze on one of the remaining merchants' tables. She scooped up a round serving tray and spun without missing a beat, hurling the plate like a discus. She managed a smile when she heard a very satisfying "ugh" as the tray found its target. One of the men went down and the other jumped over him.

Jake raced onto the pier and leaped into a nearby powerboat. Amy barely had time to get into the seat next to him before he turned the key and gunned the engine. Amy shot a glance over her shoulder. The men were struggling to break through the unruly crowd, knocking people out of their way as they made their way toward the pier.

Jake pushed the throttle to full, throwing Amy back into her seat, lashed with sea spray. He carved a path south, straight down the coast toward Tunis. Behind them, Pierce's men were through the crowd, and Amy watched as they commandeered a boat of their own.

"We're going to need a new plan!" Amy said.

"It's your turn," Jake yelled over the roar of the engines, earning himself a glare from Amy. "I came up with stealing the boat!"

The men were now less than fifty yards behind them. One of them was leaning forward, gun in hand. As soon as they were out of sight of the crowds at the marina, he began firing. Bullets zipped past Amy and Jake, splashing into the churning water around them.

The lights of Tunis were growing brighter by the second.

"If we slow down enough to get ashore, they'll be on us in no time," Amy said. She pivoted in her seat, searching for anything that might help. A little bit of land. Other ships. Anything. All she saw was a vast stretch of dark sea. "Steer us out into the open water."

"And do what? Take this thing to Italy?"

Bullets pierced the fiberglass deck behind them, slamming their way closer and closer.

"Just do it!"

Jake pulled the wheel over, aiming the boat straight out into open water ahead. The men behind overshot them and had to slow to turn around.

"Hope you've got a good follow-up idea!"

Me too, Amy thought as she dropped into her seat and started stripping off her shoes.

"What are you doing!?"

"We have to jump!"

"What!? You mean in the water?"

"It's dark," Amy said. "They won't see us. They'll follow the boat while we'll swim back to the beach."

Jake looked behind them. "Swim? We're a mile from shore!"

"Do you have a better idea?"

"Yes! It's called NOT DROWNING!"

A trio of gunshots thundered behind them. Amy stripped off her cardigan and stood by the edge of the boat. "Take off your shoes and jacket and let's go!"

"Amy!"

Amy threw her arms over her head and dove into the rushing water. As fast as they were going, it was like hitting wet concrete. She tumbled in the water end over end, plummeting into the dark beneath the waves. For a terrifying moment Amy couldn't even figure out which way was up, until she spotted air bubbles floating to the surface. Amy followed them, pulling with all her might until she exploded out of the water with a gasp. A second later there was a scream of engines and the other boat raced by.

"Jake!" Amy called into the dark after the boat had passed. "Jake!"

Amy searched frantically, but didn't see him anywhere. *What if he stayed in the boat? What if he's still out there all alone?*

"Jake!" she screamed.

Amy searched the darkness, growing more and more anxious until she heard a splash nearby. The surface broke and Jake appeared, gulping back air. Amy stroked toward him, putting one arm around his back and kicking to lift them beyond the reach of the swells of black water.

"You okay?"

Jake coughed and then he nodded weakly.

"Can you swim?"

"Yeah," he said. "I'm good. Let's go."

By the time they pulled themselves out of the surf and onto the beach, all they could do was collapse onto their backs. Amy lay there panting, the muscles in her arms and legs buzzing with exhaustion. Jake was sitting up, draped over his knees, breathing hard and shivering despite the warmth of the night. He looked like a half-drowned puppy. Amy couldn't help but smile.

"You were right," she said over the crashing waves. "I was completely lost."

Jake looked back to her, pushing the wet hair out of his eyes. She had given him a golden opportunity to rub it in. All she could do was brace herself for it.

"You were actually only about a mile or so from the

museum," he said. "You would have gotten there."

In the wet chill, Jake's smile felt as warm as a bonfire.

"Come on," Amy said. "Let's get out of here. Maybe if we're lucky, Dan's found that pizza."

Amy started to go but Jake took hold of her wrist.

"Back in the medina. Going after that guy . . . it was one of the stupidest things I've ever done in my life. I wasn't thinking. I just wanted to *do* something. You know?"

"Yeah," she said. "I do."

Twenty minutes after they found a taxi willing to take two sopping-wet teenagers, Jake and Amy pulled up in front of their hotel.

"Hey, look," Amy said, pointing out the window. "It's Dan and Atticus."

The two of them were just coming up the sidewalk as Jake and Amy left the cab.

"Whoa!" Atticus said when he saw them. "What happened to you guys?"

"What?" Jake said, mock incredulous. "We just went for a little swim."

Amy laughed. "Yeah, it was such a nice night we couldn't resist. What did we miss here?"

"We found it!" Dan exclaimed. "Tunisian pizza! And you'll never believe it. The stuff has tuna fish on it!"

"And hard-boiled eggs!" Atticus chimed in.

"At first, you think it's a crime against the pizza gods, but then you taste it and it blows your mind."

"We'll have to try some," Amy said with a doubtful look. "Att, Jake says you think we should try your father again."

"Totally," he said. "You guys want to change first or something?"

"Nah," Amy said. "We'll dry off on the way. Come on."

The four of them set off down the streets of Tunis, Amy and Jake trailing behind while Dan and Atticus took the lead, babbling excitedly about a video arcade they found down near the medina. All around them, nightclubs and cafés were buzzing. The air was warm on Amy's skin, and it smelled of the spicy aroma of roasting meats from the restaurants they passed.

For a wonderful moment, Amy felt like just another tourist, gliding through the town with her friends without a care in the world. She even found herself wishing Ian was there and Jonah and Nellie and Hamilton, too. Even Pony.

"It's just up here!" Atticus said, leading them down a quaint street lit by the glow of amber streetlights. They went halfway down the block, then opened a black gate that led up to a small two-story house.

Amy knew there was something wrong immediately. The front door was hanging wide open. Even from the sidewalk, she could see a turned-over book-case and a floor covered in papers.

"Does your dad live alone?" Amy asked.

Atticus nodded, speechless, and Amy rushed past him, up the stairs and into the house. She stood in the brightly lit front room, surveying the damage. The place had been ransacked. Coffee tables and chairs were turned on their sides and every surface was covered in papers and books and journals, all looking like they had been torn off the shelves and thrown aside randomly.

"Dr. Rosenbloom!" Amy called.

"Dad!" Jake yelled.

"I'm trying to call his cell phone, but he isn't answering," Atticus said.

"It's probably nothing," Jake said. "You know how Dad gets when he's working on something. I bet he just—"

"They saw him talking to us. They think he's involved."

Everyone turned at the sound of Amy's voice. She was staring at the floor, hating how sure she felt.

"Who did?" Jake asked. "Amy? Who saw him?"

Amy forced herself to look at Jake and Atticus. She felt something like a lump of chalk in her throat.

"Pierce's men," she said. "They've kidnapped your father."

CHAPTER 10

This is never going to work, Nellie thought as she stood in the parking lot at Trilon Laboratories. Hundreds of her soon-to-be fellow employees were streaming out of their cars and up to the building. There were so many of them! And they all seemed so full of energy and purpose. Every scrap of conversation Nellie caught was incomprehensible, full of words like *entropy* and *metalloids* and *protonation*.

Nellie waited for the flood to pass, then steadied herself with a deep breath and trooped up the stairs. Once inside, she saw that the building was surprisingly small. *I wonder how they get all those people in here?*

As Nellie crossed the entryway, she noticed the black security cameras that hung in every corner, like nesting bats. There were guards, too, men in gray uniforms with guns on their hips and radio earpieces. It was heavy security for a little pharmaceutical plant. The place was getting more suspicious by the second.

Nellie came to a security gate that led back into the labs. Next to the card reader on the gate there was a large blue D that matched the letter on Nellie's ID card. Nellie swiped her card and made her way through a maze of white hallways, looking for lab 237. Each lab she passed buzzed with small teams of scientists. She kept an eye out for Sammy, but she knew there was no way finding him was going to be easy.

Nellie's stomach flipped when she finally found herself outside lab 237. A group of five scientists stood in the middle conferring with their backs to her, spouting more science gibberish.

". . . but, Doctor, Avogadro's law clearly states that . . ."

"Someone bring me the Eppendorf tube!!"

"—great Scott, man! Think of the neutrinos!"

Every molecule in Nellie's body wanted retreat; she could never mix with these people. It didn't matter that she changed her clothes and dyed her hair. She was Nellie Gomez, not—

"Dr. Gormley!"

The five scientists were staring at her. One of them, an older man with snowy hair, crossed the room with his hand out.

"I'm Dr. Wentworth! So good to have you here. We've heard nothing but wonderful things! It'll be a pleasure to have someone who really knows what she's doing take over the lab!"

Nellie's heart skipped a beat. "Take over?"

"Yes!" Dr. Wentworth laughed. "We all heard that you came in for an assistant's position, but George

Takahashi knows talent when he sees it. He fired Dr. Carstairs and decided to give you the job!"

"Well, that's . . . that's just . . . it's *amazing*," Nellie sputtered, feeling her head spin. "But certainly there are people who would be better suited to—"

"Nonsense!" Dr. Wentworth hustled Nellie inside and to a desk at the front of the room. "With your credentials, you're going to be perfect. A breath of fresh air. Now, is there anything we can get you before we start? Coffee? Dr. Assad! Coffee for Dr. Gormey!"

"Yes, sir!" One of the other scientists dashed out of the room.

"All of us here are so eager to get started," Dr. Wentworth continued.

Nellie seized on the opportunity. "Yes! You should do that! Just go ahead and get started. Great idea!"

Dr. Wentworth stared at her blankly and then turned to a woman next to him.

"Get started doing . . . what?" the woman asked.

Nellie floundered. A huge chalkboard sat at the other end of the room, covered with equations and strange symbols. "Continuing the great work you're already doing!"

Dr. Wentworth laughed his jolly laugh. "Oh, all of Dr. Carstairs's projects were canceled when he was fired. Best thing that could have happened, really; his approach was getting us nowhere."

The woman chimed in. "Mr. Takahashi said now that you're here we can expect a radical new approach in the creation of complex dihydrate benzo protein phosphates."

"Did he!?" Nellie squeaked.

"Oh, yes! Since it was the subject of your PhD thesis."

Nellie braced herself with her palms on her desk, fighting the light-headedness that was spreading fast. The door to the lab stood open less than ten feet away. The elevators were just fifteen feet down the hall. She could be back in her car and on the road in minutes.

No! The world is counting on you, Gomez. All you have to do is get these people off your back long enough to do some snooping. Do something!

But what? The last time she had taken a chemistry class was in the eighth grade, and she hadn't paid the slightest bit of attention. She had just discovered cooking and couldn't get herself to spend more than a few minutes with her nose out of Julia Child's *Mastering the Art of French Cooking.*

But wait, Nellie thought. *Isn't cooking just chemistry?* Instead of a formula, you have a recipe. Instead of chemicals, you mix ingredients together in precise proportions until they combine and become something else. There's really no difference at all. *So what's the secret to great cooking? Think, Gomez, think!*

"Uh . . . Dr. Gormey?"

Nellie pounded her palm on the tabletop. "Salt!"

She looked up at a sea of utterly blank faces. *Did I just say that out loud?* Dr. Wentworth stepped forward.

"Uh . . . what do you mean *salt?*"

Nellie decided to go for broke. She strode to the chalkboard and picked up an eraser. She wiped away all of their equations and replaced them with *SALT* in huge letters. "That's our radical new approach, ladies and gentlemen!" she declared. "Salt! Sodium!"

"You're saying mix sodium into the formula?"

"Yes!" Nellie said. "That's exactly what I'm saying."

"But that doesn't make any sense!" one of the other scientists interrupted.

"He's right!" cried another. "If we simply add sodium to the mixture, it will destroy the whole thing!"

"And it would be highly dangerous!"

In seconds, the scientists had her completely surrounded, screeching about salt and sodium and the accepted practices in modern chemistry. The only thing to do was run. Nellie took a step toward the door just as young Dr. Assad appeared in the doorway with her coffee, a stunned look on his face at the chaos in the room.

That's when the idea hit her. *Ian!* Nellie swiped the coffee mug out of Dr. Assad's hand, took one sip, then hurled it across the room. The mug hit the far wall and exploded, sending coffee and shards of pottery flying.

"YOU CALL THIS SWILL *COFFEE*!?"

The angry chatter ceased immediately, as if someone had reached in and turned the sound off in the room. The doctors turned to her, mouths agape.

"Are you trying to poison me?" Nellie shrieked. "Is that instant? And powdered creamer? What do you think I am, an animal?"

Dr. Wentworth stepped forward. "Dr. Gormey, I—"

Nellie wheeled on Wentworth. "And you! Everyone back in my lab at Harvard said the scientists at Trilon labs were a bunch of monkey-brained hacks! I said no! All they need is a few fresh new ideas and the sky's the limit. But here I am, dropping genius at your feet, and this is how you react!? Are you all blind? Are you fools!?"

"But, Dr. Gormey—"

"Don't 'Dr. Gormey' me, Dr. Wayneworth."

"It's Wentworth actually, but—"

"I don't have time to hold your hands! I've given you the answer! Do you need me to do *all* of your work for you?"

"N-no," Dr. Wentworth stuttered. "Of course not! It's just that salt—"

"No excuses! I want reports by the end of the week. We're trying to save lives here, people!"

"Of course, Dr. Gormey!"

"And *you*," Nellie said, wheeling on a quaking Dr. Assad. "I want to see a double-caff nonfat caramel mochaccino with whipped cream on my desk in ten minutes or you're fired!"

"Yes, ma'am!"

Dr. Assad sprinted out of the room. Nellie crossed her arms and leaned against the back wall as everyone scattered to their jobs, bending over Bunsen burners. They wouldn't look up again for hours.

Being Dr. Nadine Gormey was *awesome*.

CHAPTER 11

"Amy! Amy, wait up!" Dan ran after his sister as she tore into the hotel lobby. "Why would Pierce take Dr. Rosenbloom?"

"To get to us."

"But Pierce doesn't *want* anything from us. He just wants us dead! Amy!"

Amy barreled past a trio of stunned tourists and took the stairway two steps at a time. When she got to their floor Amy ripped their hotel room door open and stomped inside, heading straight for the telephone.

"Who are you calling?"

"The police!"

Dan slapped his hand down over the receiver before Amy could pick it up. "Whoa, Amy. You know how this works. If we call the police—"

"We can't just sit here while Pierce does who knows what to their father, Dan. That's the game we played with Damien Vesper, and I'm not playing it this time."

"Amy—"

"We went to Dr. Rosenbloom for *help*, Dan."

The pain in Amy's voice was heart wrenching. As much as Dan hated to admit it, he knew she was right. They'd lost people before, and were still trying to cope. How could they take that chance again, with Atticus and Jake's own father? Dan let his hand slip off the phone and Amy grabbed it and started to dial. Before she could finish, the phone was ripped off the table and out of Amy's hand. They turned to find the phone cord clutched in Jake's fist.

"Calling the police will get him killed," Jake said. "Pierce taking him means he wants to bargain, and that gives us an opportunity. We wait to see what he has to say and then we pull one over on him."

"Jake—" Amy started.

"That's how this works," Jake said. "You know that."

"Att," Dan said. "You on board with this?"

Atticus was standing behind his brother, arms crossed over his chest, head down so his dreadlocks shadowed his face. He nodded slowly.

"So what do we do in the meantime?" Dan asked.

"Our job," Jake said with a deep, shuddering breath. "We still have to find the silphium. Atticus, go through Olivia's notebook line by line in case we missed something. Dan, see if you can find anything on the web. Amy, help me look for places in the area with a Founders Media connection. Maybe we can narrow down the places they might be holding Dad."

"We won't find him," Amy said.

"Come on, Amy," Dan said with a pale smile. "Our record for outsmarting homicidal madmen is the best in the league!"

"But Pierce is smarter than any of them," she said, looking from Dan to Jake to the still-unmoving Atticus. "Isn't he?"

The four of them spread out through the room and worked silently, hunched over papers and computer screens. Dan craved the usual chatter of their research sessions, but even he was too tense to kick it off. He couldn't stop looking over at the phone. Why didn't Pierce just call and end the waiting?

When Dan wasn't staring at the phone, he was watching Atticus. Someone who didn't know Att would probably think he was as focused as ever, but Dan saw the truth each time Atticus fumbled his pencil and on every page his friend lingered over just a second too long.

"That's it," Jake said, sitting back and rubbing his LCD-burning eyes. "I've done it. I've reached the end of the Internet."

"What's there?" Dan asked.

"Pretty much what you'd expect," he said. "A lolcat."

Jake had the right idea. Dan was fried, too. He reached across the table and flicked the TV on to an English-language news channel.

"Dan," Amy said.

"What? I just want to see how my Sox are doing. You find anything on Founders Media?"

"Nothing," Amy said. "Despite owning every other media outlet in the world — along with pharmaceutical companies and Internet start-ups — Founders Media has nothing in Tunisia."

"That can't be possible."

"It's true," Jake said. "We even had Pony do some digging back home. Pierce doesn't have any reach here. Not one that leaves a trace anyway."

"Atticus?"

"Zilch," he said, rubbing at his bloodshot eyes. "I mean, there's all kinds of stuff in here, but it's hard to figure out what's important and what's a four-hundred-year-old shopping list."

"Uh-oh!" Dan sat up in his chair and fumbled for the remote.

"What?" Amy said. "Dan, what is it?"

"Nothing!" Dan snapped the TV off. "Don't worry about it. Hey! Who wants to go break into the Tunisian national archives?"

Amy tore the remote out of his hands.

"No, Amy, wait —"

The TV came back on, showing two highly polished talking heads at a massive chrome-and-glass desk. Amy took a seat behind Dan and dropped the remote by a large crystal ashtray on the table next to her.

". . . and for more news on those globe-trotting troublemakers, Dan and Amy Cahill, we now turn to senior international crime correspondent Chet Waterdam. Chet?"

"Come on, Amy," Dan said. "We don't need to see this."

A leathery-looking man with orange skin and bright red suspenders appeared on the screen.

"Thanks, Wes. The Cahill kids! At first, we here at CVB News thought it was all fun and games, but now we have learned that what we are looking at is actually an international criminal conspiracy of staggering proportions. But first, the Cahills — who are they!?"

The dopiest picture Dan had ever seen of himself popped up on the screen.

"Dan Cahill!" Chet exclaimed. "Second in command. A fanatically loyal but weak-willed and dim-witted hanger-on."

"Hey!" cried Dan.

"The real power of the Cahill cabal rests here."

Dan's picture was replaced by a grainy one of Amy at the mouth of a seedy-looking street in some unnamed city, looking mysterious and furtive.

AMY CAHILL

"Amy Cahill! A reckless thrill junkie in the guise of a librarian in training."

"Well, they got you there," Dan said, hoping for a laugh, but getting a glare instead.

"Ms. Cahill is cruel. Never willing to get her own hands dirty, though, she has a history of luring boys into doing her bidding."

The TV screen filled with a shot of a smiling Evan, standing in the sun. Dan looked back at Amy. She was transfixed, eyes wide, skin pale.

EVAN TOLLIVER

"Amy," he said. "Seriously. Turn it off."

"Evan Tolliver," the voice-over intoned. "Brilliant student and beloved son of Terrence and Letitia Tolliver.

But why don't we let *them* tell you about him . . ."

Evan's picture faded, replaced by a gray-haired man in a white T-shirt and a woman in a prim blue dress. They were sitting side by side on a sunlit porch with a farm stretching out behind them.

"Our son loved Amy Cahill," Letitia Tolliver said in a pain-racked voice. "He loved her more than anything."

Terrence Tolliver drew his wife close as she pulled off her glasses to wipe a single tear from her cheek.

"That's right," Terrence said. "He loved her and she killed him. Sure as if the girl had held the gun in her own hand. She drew him into her world, and this poor boy, our only son, never made it out alive. And she runs around the world like she doesn't have a care."

"Amy . . ." Jake said, but even he went quiet as the camera moved closer to Mr. Tolliver's face. He and his wife each looked far older than they used to. An off-camera voice spoke up.

"And what would your message be to anyone associating with Ms. Cahill now?"

"Get away from that girl as fast as you can," Letitia said. "She looks innocent, but she's a snake."

Amy was motionless, leaning forward in her chair. In the flickering light of the TV, her eyes were dark hollows.

"Strong words," Chet continued. "Ones that lead to perhaps the most important question of all — has Amy Cahill already found her next victim?"

The screen faded to another picture. It was Jake,

caught standing in that medina alley. He wore an angry sneer and his fist was cocked, ready to strike the reporter who sat bleeding at his feet. Amy stood in the shadows behind him, watching it all with a look on her face that, had Dan not known her, he would have read as distinctly pleased.

"Jake Rosenbloom—star athlete, honors student, a young man with a bright future ahead of him. How long until Amy Cahill takes all that away, too? For more on this—"

Something zipped through the air by Dan's head and the TV screen exploded in a shower of glass and plastic and electrical sparks. Dan jumped out of his seat as a crystal ashtray hit the floor and shattered. Dan turned to see Amy standing at the edge of the table with tears in her eyes.

"It's Pierce that's doing this," Dan said. "You know that. This is meaningless."

"It's not meaningless to me!" Amy cried. "Maybe you can just run away, Dan, but I can't. I have to stay! I have to deal with this!"

"I'm not running away!"

"I must have been crazy," Amy said. "I don't know why I thought this would work. Dan, call the pilot. Tell him he's taking Jake and Atticus home. Tonight."

"Amy," Jake said. "You can't think I believe any of this."

Amy whirled on him. "It doesn't matter what you believe! We are done talking about this. Dan and I will find the silphium and the police will find your father and that's it."

"No," Jake said. "Amy, that's not how this is going to work."

"This is crazy," Dan said. "You can't expect them to—"

"That is an order!" Amy roared.

Dan felt himself knocked backward, the sting of Amy's words like a punch. Everyone in the room went silent. They were like four statues, frozen in opposite corners of the room, muscles tense as steel, vibrating with anger.

"I am the leader of the Cahills," Amy said, her deadly calm more frightening than a scream. "I don't want to hear any more thoughts or any more discussion. This is how it's going to be and that's it."

Before anyone could say another word, Amy threw open the door to her bedroom and slammed it behind her.

Jake and Dan and Atticus didn't move.

"Dan," Jake said. "You have to talk to her."

Dan nodded but he didn't turn back to Jake or Atticus, he just kept staring at the smashed TV.

CHAPTER 12

Amy sat on the floor of her shower, searing water falling over her head and shoulders and filling the room with steam. She had turned the water so hot, her skin was red and aching, but she couldn't stop shivering.

The faces of Evan's parents haunted her. It was as if they had been printed with phosphorescent ink on the back of her eyelids, inescapable no matter how hard she tried to block them out. For so long, Amy had drowned out the guilt that raged inside her with the voices of all of the people who told her that it wasn't her fault. That Evan knew the risks.

Now a few words from Evan's parents, and the wound was raw again. Evan had gotten involved because of his feelings for her. Amy could have stopped him, but she hadn't.

Amy shut the water off and went into her bedroom, wrapped in a towel. It was quiet on the other side of the door. She could only imagine what the boys must have said when she left the room. What they must think of her. Amy fell across her bed just as her cell phone began to ring. She wanted to ignore it, but the caller ID showed up as coming from Attleboro. She took a breath and made herself answer it.

"We're thinking it must be drugs."

Amy almost smiled with relief at the rich lilt of Ian Kabra's voice.

"Some sort of truth serum–like compound—"

"But not one that makes you tell the truth!" Hamilton shouted in the background.

"I said truth serum–*like*, Hamilton. Now please, I'm trying to talk. *Tomas*," Ian grumbled and then turned back to the phone. "We think Pierce must have slipped some kind of will-weakening drug into their water so when the reporter suggested what he wanted the Tollivers to say, they said it. Simple, really."

Amy was on her back, staring at the pressed-tin ceiling. The heat from the shower had dissipated and a chill was snaking up her legs. She felt distant from herself, like she was watching from above.

"Amy?" Ian said. "Amy, are you there?"

"It wasn't drugs," she said.

"You can't believe that these people would honestly think—"

"How often do you think about Natalie?"

Now it was Ian's turn to go silent. Amy's ear was filled with the soft in and out of his breathing.

"I don't think it's appropriate to . . ." he started with his usual brusque energy but then his voice faltered. "I think about her all the time," he admitted.

Amy turned onto her side, pressing the phone between her ear and the pillow.

"But sometimes is it like you . . ." Amy struggled with an idea that seemed to retreat from her even as she grabbed at it. "Forget?"

"Forget what?"

"That she's really gone? Like one day you'll just turn a corner and" — Amy's voice caught in her throat but she pressed on — "she'll be there? Or you'll look at other people and for a second you see her in their place."

"I hear her voice sometimes," Ian confessed. "I mean I think I do. There's always this split second when I think, *Oh, no, what does she want me to do now?* but then I catch myself."

"I guess that's what other people don't get. That people who are gone aren't really gone."

"No," Ian said. "They never are."

A lump grew in Amy's throat.

"Yo, Ian!"

Amy could hear a scuffle for the phone.

"Jonah! Unhand me!"

"Go get me a spot of tea, old man," Jonah said in his best Ian impression. "Gotta holler at the boss a minute."

Amy heard Ian harrumph and then Jonah's swaggering voice filled her ear.

"Yo! Amy K-to-the-Hill."

"Hi, Jonah," Amy said. "How are things there?"

"Never mind that. This is wisdom-dropping time. What those two said on TV was cold."

"I really don't want to—"

"I know. I know. I'm not here to discuss your feelings. I'm here to make a knowledge deposit."

"Oh, yeah, and what's that?"

"All those people crowding around you with cameras and little notebooks? Those *reporters*." Jonah said the word with obvious disgust. "They are nothing but dogs looking for a bone to chew on."

"Well, unfortunately that bone is us."

"Yeah, but it doesn't have to be. See, all a dog wants is something between its teeth. It doesn't care what it is. Reporters are the same way. All they're trying to do is make a buck by keeping a lot of bored people entertained."

"So what are you saying?"

"I'm saying that if you want a dog to drop one bone, all you gotta do is give him a new one."

"And how am I supposed to do that?"

"When I want to get reporters off my back, I call in an anonymous tip that Justin Bieber is getting a crew cut on the other side of town."

"Somehow I don't think they're going to buy that over here."

"I don't know, Cahill, that little dude gets around."

Amy surprised herself by laughing. "All right. Thanks, Jonah. I'll see what I can do."

"Hard-won knowledge, Amy. Hard. Won."

Amy said good-bye to Jonah and then stared at the door. She couldn't hide in here forever. Amy got dressed, then stood with her hand on the doorknob listening to the quiet shuffle of Dan and Atticus and Jake on the other side. Her stomach did flips as she remembered the sound of her voice as she barked orders at them.

You did what you had to do, Amy told herself. *What you should have done long ago.*

Amy caught her breath and forced herself through the door. No one said a word, but every head in the room turned as Amy stepped through the door. Jake was down on one knee by the bed, stuffing clothes into a gym bag. Dan sat by the window, watching her with a kind of guarded interest. The way you'd look at a stranger before you've decided if they're friend or foe.

"I didn't call the plane," he announced. "We don't have the right to tell Jake and Atticus to go."

"But don't worry, Your Leaderhood," Jake said. "We're leaving. Atticus and I will stay at Dad's place while we keep looking for him. You and Dan can find the silphium. When something comes in from Pierce on Dad, Dan will forward it to me."

All Amy could do was nod. This was what she wanted, wasn't it? She caught a glimmer of glass on the rug by the TV, and the buzz of nerves in her stomach swelled.

"I've been going over Olivia's journal," Atticus said. He sat by the door, Olivia's notebook in front of him, his own bag at his feet. He turned the notebook around and showed it to her. He pointed at a shiny smudge at the top corner of one page.

"You remember we were eating lunch? Well, that's the last grease smudge from his thumb, so this is where Dad stopped right before he ran out. I thought maybe he saw something about the silphium but . . ."

Amy studied a jumble of what looked like names. *Critias. Timaeus. Hermocrates.* At the bottom there was a single sentence. *The twentieth Hafsid claims to keep the testament of the failed strategoi.*

"What does it all mean?"

"Well, the sentence is gibberish to me," Atticus said. "But the first three are names."

"Who are they?"

"Nobody," he said. "Like *literally* nobody. They're characters Plato used in his dialogues."

"Dialogues?" Dan said. "This guy was a playwright?"

"No, Plato was a classical Greek philosopher around the fourth century B.C. The dialogues were a literary form he used. Instead of him writing a book explaining his ideas, he'd create characters and have them discuss stuff. These three were the main speakers in a projected trilogy of dialogues."

"Projected?"

"Plato completed the first one, called *Timaeus*. The second one, *Critias*, was half done. *Hermocrates* was supposed to be the third, but he never wrote it."

"Makes sense," Dan said. "Sequels are never as good as the original."

Amy couldn't help but smile. She looked back at Dan, but he turned away as soon as their eyes met.

"So why'd your dad get so freaked by it?"

"No idea," Atticus said. "And I don't see any connection to silphium, either. Plato's dialogues never mention it, and they never even talk about Carthage."

Jake grabbed his bag and turned to Atticus. "Come on, bro. We should get moving."

Atticus handed the notebook over to Amy and then slung his bag over his shoulder. "Good luck," he said. "See ya, Dan."

"Yeah," Dan said, fighting back the emotion Amy could hear in his voice. "See ya, Att."

It's for the best, Amy thought. *One day they'll understand.*

Jake and Atticus started to go, but before they could leave, there was a crisp knock on the door.

"Excuse me, please," came a harried man's voice from the other side of the door. "This is the hotel manager. I am most embarrassed but we have just been informed of a small fire on the top floors of the building. We must ask that all residents evacuate immediately."

"A fire?" Dan said.

Jake quickly backtracked to the window. "Guys," he said. "Look."

"Just a moment!" Amy said to the manager, and crossed the room.

Jake pulled aside the curtain and nodded out into the dark. "I'm not from around here," he said. "But those sure don't look like fire trucks to me."

Several nondescript cars and a large minivan loitered below. All were black and seemed to have more than the usual amount of antennas and lights. Bulky men in suits stood around smoking cigarettes and keeping a sharp eye all around.

"If there's one thing I've learned in the last year," Jake said, "it's that no matter where you go, cops pretty much look the same."

"That's all for us?" Dan asked.

"We're the Cahill kids," Amy said. "International criminals."

"Stealing that boat probably didn't help," Jake said.

Dan looked at Amy. "You guys stole a boat?"

"It's not just cops, either," Amy said.

She pointed to another cluster of men. They were mixing with the Tunisian police but they were Westerners, broad shouldered and lean with crisp military haircuts. Official-looking badges hung around their necks, but Amy knew they weren't the Feds.

"Pierce's men?" Dan asked.

Amy nodded. "Probably pretending to be FBI or US Marshals."

"Excuse me!" the manager called again, his accented voice slurring with panic. "Miss! It is most important that you come down to the lobby immediately. This fire, it is very dangerous!"

"What do we do?" Atticus asked.

He looked to Amy and something locked up inside

of her. "Maybe . . . maybe we go with him. Once we're out we slip away, go out the back . . ."

"The other hotel exits will be covered by now," Jake said. "Besides, he's probably got cops standing right next to him. Atticus, block the door and get our things!"

Atticus stuck a chair under the door handle and grabbed their backpacks. Jake hit the light switch and the hotel room went dark.

"What are you doing?" Amy asked.

"Dan, give me a hand!"

Jake pulled the window shades open and then Dan rushed over to help. The window was heavy, but with a giant yank, it flew open and a hot gust of wind blew into the room. There was a thin concrete shelf just below the window that encircled the building.

"Miss, please!" the manager pleaded. "The fire, it is quite big now!"

There was a click as the manager unlocked the door, and then a thump as he tried to open it. Jake grabbed the windowsill and climbed up onto the ledge.

"Jake, wait!" Amy said. "We can't!"

But Dan was already following him out, with Atticus close behind. A wall-shaking boom came from behind her as someone began trying to break the door down. There was no other choice. Amy leaped up onto the windowsill and out into the night.

CHAPTER 13

Pony was deep in the jungle and there were tigers everywhere.

He could feel their eyes on him at every turn, crouching at the edge of firewalls and lurking, ravenous, within system registries. Pony had no doubt that he was one of the very best, but Founders Media had withstood years of attacks from everyone from Anonymous to Mafiaboy and possibly to April May herself. It wouldn't give up its secrets without a bloody fight, hence the tigers — sentries made of code ready to pounce if he made one wrong move.

As soon as Pony had seen the last news story from Founders Media, he knew he had to try something. He started by reaching into relatively unprotected file servers and deleting articles and photo and video files. They always came back, though, sometimes within minutes.

His newest gambit was to delve deep within Founders Media's internal servers. He wasn't quite sure what the endgame was — maybe to find info to implicate Pierce in the attacks against Amy and Dan. Maybe do deep and serious damage to his network. First, Pony needed to get in. And that was proving much harder than he'd thought.

Pony pushed the keyboard away. His head was pounding. His eyeballs ached. There was only one cure for what ailed him. Pony left his station in the command center and walked back to the kitchen in a post-hacking haze. Around him, Hamilton, Ian, and Jonah were bent over books and computers of their own, poking at a hundred different mysteries.

"Hey, Pony," Hamilton said.

"Pony Boy!" Jonah said. "You staying gold?"

Pony still couldn't quite believe that Jonah Wizard was actually talking to him.

"Just taking a break. How's the research going?"

Jonah swiveled around in his chair. "Huge! Me and Ham here broke this whole thing wide open."

"No way."

"Check it out," Jonah said. "We learned that the desert outside Tunis was used as a primary location for the first Star Wars movie. And not only that, so was Tikal in Guatemala."

"And," Hamilton said, "Angkor Wat was used as a model for a planet briefly mentioned in *Revenge of the Sith*."

Pony looked at them blankly. "So?"

Hamilton leaned forward. "So we have to ask ourselves," he said in a conspiratorial whisper, "have we fully considered George Lucas's role in all of this?"

Pony rolled his eyes. "You two need anything from the fridge?"

Hamilton shook his head.

"Big glass," Jonah said. "Half ginger ale. Half root beer."

"Ian?"

Ian ignored him, which was no surprise. He'd barely said a word since they'd gotten back to Attleboro. He sat in a dark alcove staring at a computer screen or pacing angrily downstairs. Pony figured that being benched must be driving him crazy.

Pony rooted around in the fridge until he found his magic elixir. Electroshock Cherry Limeade Caffeine Blast. Pony didn't bother with a glass; he upended the two liter and let it slosh out of the bottle and down his throat. He imagined his life bar go from caution red to yellow to a glowing electric green. He grabbed a second two liter and Jonah's drink, then headed back to his station.

"What's up, Pony?"

Pony almost spit out a mouthful of soda. Nellie was sitting in his chair, but there was something distinctly un-goddesslike about her.

"You look . . . weird."

"You know, Pony, I think it's your tact that makes everyone love you so much."

"But your hair. And your clothes. You're dressed like my mom."

Nellie's brown eyes narrowed on him. "I'm

undercover," she growled. "Now sit down. I need your help."

"What's up?"

"I need anything you can get me on Trilon Laboratories."

This was music to Pony's ears. Nellie moved out of his chair and he leaned into his keyboard like a musician, his fingers be-bopping over the keys, pounding out a crisp plastic rhythm. In the end the whole thing was a bit of a disappointment. Pony shrugged and took another swig of his hacker juice. "There."

"There what?"

"Pwnage. Total and complete pwnage."

"I really need some kind of geek-to-English dictionary."

"I'm in," Pony said. "Right in the middle of their systems. Trilon Laboratories now officially works for me."

"Already?"

"It was just off-the-shelf security stuff. Easy to break."

"So what's there?"

Pony surfed the system, dipping in and out of files at will. "Not much. E-mail. Some accounting stuff. A list of all fifty-seven employees."

"Wait. Fifty-seven? I saw like a hundred people in the parking lot."

Pony surfed around until he could bring up a rough schematic of the building. "In here? They'd need a crowbar to fit that many people in a building this size."

"Can you print that out?"

One keystroke and a full set of blueprints were spooling through the printer. Pony spread them out on a table and pored over lines and notation.

"Anything weird?" Nellie asked.

"It appears to be a building," Pony said. "With walls and a floor. And a roof."

Nellie glared at him.

"What? Paper isn't really my strong suit."

Nellie pushed him out of the way and traced the maze of lines in and out of rooms. She turned a page to look at the electrical wiring schematics.

"Huh," she said. "Look."

Pony sat forward, flipping the pages back and forth. He would never have thought it possible with something as supremely lame as some sheets of paper, but he started to feel that familiar hacking feeling. It was like he was melting into the data, becoming one with it, losing himself. For a flash of a second, Pony was those blueprints.

"Do you see it?" Nellie asked.

"It's like there are two buildings," Pony said. "Look at the basement. The walls and the ceiling are super thick, way heavier than anything else upstairs, like they're blast walls or something. And it's got like an entirely separate electrical system. And look at all of the elevators and staircases."

Nellie stared down at them but shook her head. "I don't see anything."

"They don't actually go down into the basement," he said. "With all the people you said were there, you'd think they'd make sure there were plenty of ways to get downstairs but they don't. The elevator shafts and the stairways all stop at the first floor. Except for this one." Pony pointed out what looked like another stairwell. "That one goes all the way down."

Nellie thought back to wandering the halls on her way to her lab, trying to match her memories with the blue and white lines before her. "I've never seen stairs there."

"No surprise," Pony said. "According to the plans, they lead right up to a solid wall. There's no entrance or exit into that stairwell on any floor but the basement."

"I'm guessing we should put that in the suspicious column," Nellie said as she gathered the plans. "Good work."

Nellie gave him a sisterly sock on the arm and headed out with the plans under her arm. Watching her go, Pony felt that deflated feeling he usually got after disconnecting from a serious day of hacking. It was strange. Pony had always been a loner. A keyboard jockey in a dank basement living on Electroshock and anchovy-and-pineapple pizza. But now he was part of a team.

There's no way I'm letting these people down.

Pony pulled up to his computer and took another slug of Electroshock.

"Time to go to war, Founders Media," he said, cracking his knuckles one by one. "Brace yourself for ultimate pwnage."

CHAPTER 14

Amy's clothes snapped like flags in the wind out on the ledge. She dared a quick look down and instantly regretted it. The concrete sidewalk four stories below seemed to have an almost magnetic pull.

With Jake in the lead, the four of them inched toward a ladder that led to the roof. They kept their backs plastered to the wall, the tips of their toes dangling over the crumbly stone. So far the police down below hadn't noticed them, but they were still pounding away at the hotel room door. It was only a matter of time before they got in.

She took another shuffling step and Atticus faltered beside her, one foot slipping off the edge. Amy threw an arm over his chest, flattening him against the wall. She could feel his heart pounding beneath her fingertips. Amy gave him a weak smile.

"It's okay," she whispered. "Look."

Up ahead, Jake grabbed the ladder and pulled himself onto it. Amy's relief only lasted a second. There was a wooden crash behind her as their hotel room door shattered. The police had made it inside.

"Stop where you are!" a police officer yelled, leaning out the window.

"Go!" Amy said, and pushed Atticus ahead of her. Jake was scrambling up the ladder now and Dan was almost to it.

"You!" the officer shouted. "Down below! Lights!"

Spotlights exploded from the street. Amy held up a hand to block them and saw that Pierce's men had broken from the others and were storming into the hotel.

Dan jumped onto the ladder and pulled Atticus on behind him. With a quick prayer Amy threw herself onto the metal rungs. There was more shouting below them now, and the sound of more vehicles arriving. She was nearly to the top when one hand, greased with sweat, slipped. Gravity dug in and tried to pull her back, but Dan's hand snapped onto her wrist, holding her steady. Amy pulled herself over the edge and onto the dark roof.

"It won't be long before they're up here," Dan said.

Amy scanned the rooftop. There was a doorway in a far corner she figured led to a stairwell back down into the hotel. "We fake them out," Amy said. "Go back down, then—"

"Hey! Over here."

Amy and the others joined Jake. He had crawled his way across the roof and was at the southern edge of the hotel. They were ten stories up now, with all of

Tunis stretched out below. It was a densely packed city, one rooftop bleeding into the next, like a series of steps heading straight down to the tangle of the medina.

Jake looked over his shoulder at Dan, who shrugged, then backed away from the edge and dropped into a runner's stance.

"Whoa!" Amy said. "Jake, we can't—"

Two police officers blew through the door on the roof, guns drawn. "You there! Stop where you are!"

Dan broke into a run.

"Dan, no!"

Dan sprinted past her. His right foot hit the top of the stone wall and launched his body into the air, sailing over the three-foot gap to the next building. Amy leaped up to see him hit the rooftop hard and roll away. Jake followed, but Atticus was hanging back, clearly terrified. The police were halfway across the roof. They'd be on them in seconds. Insane or not, it was their only chance. Amy grabbed Atticus's hand and together they raced toward the edge of the roof.

Amy's foot touched the wall and she threw herself as hard as she could into the open air. Atticus did the same, and for a second they were both weightless, hurtling across space hand in hand.

Amy hit the roof of the opposite building shoulder-first and rolled away. Pain shot through her side but she ignored it, turning back to look for Atticus. He wasn't beside her.

"Atticus!"

The fingers of one small hand grasped the edge of the roof. Amy raced over and grabbed Atticus's wrist, his small body twisting over the concrete below. Amy tried to muscle him over the edge, but his skin was sweaty with fear and he started to slip. She scrambled for a better hold, but he was slipping fast and pulling her along with him.

Then she felt something behind her, a hand grabbing her shirt and pulling. She looked back. Dan. Jake appeared beside her, grasping at Atticus's other arm. Together, the three of them hauled Atticus up and over the edge. He hit the tar paper panting and Jake threw his arms around him.

"You there! Don't move!"

The police were at the edge of the hotel's roof. Jake pulled Atticus to his feet, and a second later they were all up and running. Behind them, Amy heard a cop shout something in Arabic into his radio. Amy grunted as they jumped onto the next roof. Dan landed and then ran beside her, dodging skylights and exhaust columns. He spared a look back. The two cops were still on the hotel's roof.

"Guess they just don't have the skills of the amazing flying Cahills," Dan said.

"Ha!" Atticus said. "Maybe you should try out to be an acrobat instead of a clown."

"Keep going!" Jake said. "There's no way they can keep up with us from down there. We're home free, unless of course they have a —"

The scream of a helicopter's rotors hit them a

fraction of a second before its searchlight switched on and erased the night around them.

"You are under arrest!"

There was nothing to do but keep running. The four jumped from building to building until the muscles in Amy's legs were screaming. The buildings got lower as they neared the medina. First six stories, then five, then four. But no matter how fast they ran or the clever turns they took, the tight ring of the helicopter's searchlight stayed fixed on them.

"There!" Dan cried.

Dan sprinted for a fire escape and they all followed. They made it down the ladder and dropped into a tight alleyway behind the buildings. The helicopter's beam was still on them, but now it was fractured by full clotheslines and fire escapes and loaded dumpsters. The four kids found a patch of shadow and disappeared into it. The plaza that led into the medina lay straight ahead.

"They have to figure that's where we're headed," Jake said.

"No choice!" Amy said. "Lots of those streets are covered, so it gets us away from the helicopter."

"Is that an order?" Jake asked.

Amy's stomach clenched. "Jake—"

"It's a maze in there, Amy! One they know a lot better than we do. One wrong turn and we end up at a dead end and they've got us."

"No," Dan said. "Amy's right. The medina's the only way."

Amy shot a quick look at her brother. "Can you do it?"

Dan stared out into the night. Amy could feel him engaging that photographic memory of his.

"I don't know," he said. "I think I remember the basic layout but—"

"It'll be enough," Amy said, legs moving like pistons. "You take the lead."

They didn't head straight to the medina. Instead they dodged around in the narrow alleys, until the searchlight slipped off them and the chop of the blades faded.

"Okay," Dan said. "Now!"

They ran out of the alley and toward the square that surrounded the entrance to the medina. They made it into the mouth of the main road and followed it for a few turns. Sirens began to wail out in the square. Amy prayed the vehicles were too big to make it into the cramped streets.

Dan led them on a wild race through unimaginably tangled streets. As they moved deeper into the medina, it was as if he were tying them into knots and untying them over and over again.

Amy heard a metallic radio squawk to her left, and then a pack of bodies moved fast down an adjoining street. Dan pulled them into an alleyway and they crouched behind trash cans as booted footsteps sped up the stone path. Amy held her breath when the boots stopped at the mouth of the alley, her pulse racing. Jake, Atticus, and Dan were hunched down, curled into balls, trying to make themselves invisible. At their backs was a solid wall of stone. No escape.

Flashlights flared, sending knife-like beacons of light over the piles of trash and debris in the alley. Jake flattened himself just seconds before one of the beams would have illuminated his arm.

The men talked low in Arabic. A radio screeched loudly. Boot heels turned on the gritty road and the men walked back the way they had come.

Amy tried to swallow, but her mouth had gone as dry as the desert. Jake went to stand, but Amy touched his back and he paused. She counted out a long and painful five minutes. When she was done, she peeked her head up cautiously, emerged from her hiding place, and approached the end of the alley.

The helicopter buzzed the tops of the buildings, its searchlight scorching the street in front of her. Once the beam passed, Amy steadied herself and moved out onto the street.

She didn't make it two steps before an icy ring of steel pressed into her temple. A deep voice boomed at the opposite end of the black handgun.

"Out of the alley, Amy. Slow."

There was a rustle of movement behind her, but Amy lifted one hand back into the dark to keep the others in their place. Her legs felt heavy and thick, unwilling to move, but she couldn't let Pierce's men come into the alley and see the others. She made herself take a step forward.

Thin moonlight illuminated four men in her peripheral vision. Westerners in black suits, all with the steel-spring bodies of Olympic athletes. The gun barrel at her temple never wavered.

"Where are the others?" the voice beside her asked.

"We split up," Amy said, trying to keep her voice steady. "About a half mile back."

One of Pierce's men ran down the street to check it out.

"What are you kids doing here?" he asked.

"Going to discos," Amy said.

There was a click as the man pulled the gun's hammer back and pushed the barrel hard into her skull. Amy flinched and bit back a scream. Her skin throbbed where the gun touched her. Her knees went weak but she refused to go down. There was another rustle in the dark of the alley and Amy motioned frantically behind her back to warn the others to stay hidden.

"You do not want to joke with me," the man with the gun said. He stepped to the side, keeping the gun pressed to her skull, and Amy caught sight of him for the first time.

She knew him. His eyes were cold and blue. Amy glanced behind him. One of the other men was holding not a gun, but a pair of handcuffs. The other had what she thought was a Taser. Something about that seemed strange. Amy struggled through her fear to grasp what was bothering her. *Only one of them has a gun. There's no one around. Nothing to stop him from pulling the trigger. So why am I still alive?* And then it clicked.

"If you were going to kill me," she said, "you would have done it already."

She expected a reaction, but the blue-eyed man didn't speak, didn't move. Amy decided to test the theory. She stepped away from him, finding her breath without the ring of steel against her temple.

"You have to make it look like an accident," she said, terrified but taking another step anyway. The man tracked her, also stepping toward the mouth of the alley.

"Don't you?" Amy insisted. "Like on the bridge in New York. *Cahill Kids Murdered* doesn't make a good headline, does it? Raises a lot of questions."

Amy kept moving backward and the man followed, his gun falling almost imperceptibly. His team followed, too. Amy prayed that some shred of her and Dan's old teamwork still existed, that her brother would guess what she was trying to do.

Amy was just a few feet from the back of the alley. She moved to take another step back, but this time the gun rose again, pointing at her forehead, dead center. The man's finger curled around the black trigger and Amy's heart missed a beat.

"How about this headline?" he said. *"Cahill Kids*

Wander into Dark Alley. Shot by Local Criminals. Bet people will believe that."

"Please," Amy said, raising her hands, trying to control her breathing, trying to stay calm. "Whatever you do with me, just let Dr. Rosenbloom go. He doesn't have anything to do with this. I swear. If you want a hostage, let him go and I'll take his place."

"Take whose place?"

"Mark Rosenbloom!"

The man's eyes narrowed and his head tilted to one side. "Who's Mark Rosenbloom?"

"AAAAAHHHHHH!"

Jake exploded out of the alley, swinging a plank of wood. It smacked into the man's wrist and the gun fell. Jake didn't miss a beat. He swung again, hitting the back of the man's head with everything he had. The board shattered and the man went down to his knees. Dan and Atticus were right behind him, a heavy steel trash can between them. They hurled it through the air and caught one of the others in the stomach. He doubled over and the Taser clattered to the street.

Amy dove for the Taser and jammed it into the third man's side as he came at her. There was a crackle and spark and the man hit the ground, flopping like a dying fish.

"Run!" she yelled.

The others joined Amy as she took off down the street. She looked over her shoulder. The three men were groggy but already starting to pick themselves up.

"This way!"

Dan jerked to the right, leading them down another twist. Amy's mind raced. Pierce's men were so much faster. They had only minutes before her energy gave out to the point that running became stumbling and falling. Maybe she could distract Pierce's men for a few seconds with a surprise melee, but fighting them head-on was hopeless.

A cramp tore into her side as she ran. Amy gasped and her hand went to it, under her jacket. She felt something stiff and square in her pocket. The idea hit her with the impact of a gunshot.

"We need a place to hide," she yelled up to Dan.

Dan turned through road after road in the dark until he came to another alley and ran into it.

Thank God for that memory of his! thought Amy.

The kids fell to their knees in the dark, out of breath. Amy listened but didn't hear the pounding of the mercenaries' boots. They had lost them, but she knew it wouldn't last. They had bought themselves seconds. If that.

"Dan," she said. "What's the fastest route back to the Bab el Bahr?"

"But that's right out in the open!" Jake said. "Amy! What are you doing?"

Amy pulled out her phone and then dug in her jacket pocket.

"Throwing our dog a new bone."

CHAPTER 15

Dan watched as his sister made a half dozen phone calls and then stuffed her phone back in her pocket.

"You sure this is going to work?" he whispered. Amy looked over at him but didn't say anything. Dan swallowed. He could see it in her eyes. This was a Hail Mary pass. He had trusted his sister without question, but she'd been so erratic lately. Was she acting rationally?

"Here they come," Jake whispered.

Every muscle in Dan's body tensed as Pierce's men turned the corner. Dan held his breath as they ran past. They were like Greek statues in motion, tireless, invulnerable. The instant their footsteps faded, Amy nodded to Jake and he sprang into the road.

"Hey!" Jake shouted. "What's the matter? You jerks can't catch a couple of kids!?"

"Go," Amy said.

Dan burst out of the alley with Amy and Atticus right behind him. He turned a sharp right and headed up the street, following the map in his head to the Bab el Bahr. There was a crash behind him as Jake pushed an empty merchant's cart into the street. It would only slow the men down for a second. Once again, he prayed his sister knew what she was doing.

Dan took another sharp turn. The plaza surrounding the Bab el Bahr was in sight. He rocketed toward it but then there was a clatter on stone and a deep *oof* behind him. Dan turned to see Jake sprawled out on the pavement, Pierce's men breaking over him like a wave.

"Jake!" Dan cried as he skidded to a stop. "Amy!"

Dan started for Jake but Amy's hand clamped onto his arm, holding him back.

"What are you—"

"We have to keep going!"

"We can't leave him!"

She yanked Dan back toward her. "Go! Now!"

Amy grabbed Atticus's arm, too, and pulled them all down the street. Dan looked back and saw the blue-eyed man hauling Jake off the ground. The Bab el Bahr and the plaza surrounding it were dead ahead. Behind them, Pierce's men were in pursuit, dragging Jake along with them. The moonlight glinted off the gun in one of their hands.

Amy didn't stop until they were at the foot of the gate. She searched the empty streets around them, her eyes wide, desperate. "They didn't come!" she said, her eyes frantic. "Why didn't they come?"

"This little chase is over."

Amy, Dan, and Atticus turned to find Pierce's men

in a semicircle around them, with Jake on his knees beside the blue-eyed man. The man had the jet-black automatic pointed at the back of Jake's head.

"A quick surrender will be the easiest for all of you," the leader said.

"And then what?" Amy asked, stepping forward. "We fall off a building? What makes the best news?"

The man lifted his gun from Jake's back and pointed it at Amy's chest. "No more time for games."

His finger tensed on the trigger but before he could fire, the sound of voices came from all directions. The square was dark, but the voices got louder and louder, as if there were a stampede on the way. Floodlights pierced the darkness.

"Amy! Dan! Over here!"

Amy pulled a stack of business cards from her pocket and threw them at the man's feet.

"Nope, it's just time for a new game," she said. "Hope you like it."

Seconds later they were surrounded on all sides by jostling reporters, nearly thirty of them, pushing and elbowing their way forward. Flashes went off like fire-crackers over their heads. In the distance, Dan could see vans with spotlights tearing into the square.

Pierce's men were surrounded. Their muscles tensed and nostrils flared as guns, Tasers, and handcuffs disappeared in their jackets. One of them even pulled Jake back up to his feet and threw an arm around him, like they were old friends.

My sister's a genius, Dan thought. *My sister is an unbelievable genius.*

"Amy! Dan!" one of the reporters shouted. "Tell us what you're doing in Tunis!"

"Any response to the Tolliver interview?"

"Is Jake Rosenbloom your new boyfriend!?"

"Dan? Why do you do whatever your sister tells you?"

The reporters fell into silence as Amy stepped into the harsh lights.

"You're asking the wrong questions!" Amy announced to the crowd of reporters. "It doesn't matter who my boyfriend is and it doesn't matter how I feel about what the Tollivers said. What matters is what's happening right here and right now. What matters is these men!" She threw an accusing finger at Pierce's men, and the reporters' heads swiveled in their direction. Pierce's men fumbled around, clearly unsure what would make their boss more angry—fighting or running.

"You need to ask yourself why men with guns are chasing a bunch of kids in the middle of the night!" Amy went on, her voice ringing out over the clicking cameras. "You need to ask why, when barely anyone had ever heard of any of us before, we're suddenly in the news every single day! Who benefits from that, and why?"

"Who, Amy?" a reporter shouted. "Who's after you!?"

Amy stood tall in the glare of the lights. Dan could feel the tension building around them until it felt like it was going to explode. He took his sister's arm and started to draw her back from the cameras, but she pulled away from him.

"The person you need to be investigating is their boss!" she said. "The man who pays them to chase us all over the world. The same man who kidnapped an innocent scholar named Dr. Mark Rosenbloom!"

"Who!?" a woman in a red suit cried. "Tell us who!"

"J. Rutherford Pierce!" yelled Amy.

It was as if a bomb went off in the middle of the plaza. Every reporter began to shout, surging forward in a tidal wave. They blew past Dan and Amy and went right for Pierce's men. Dan almost laughed to see the look of abject terror on the blue-eyed man's face. Pierce may have turned him into the most lethal killing machine the world had ever known, but nothing could prepare him for an onslaught like this. Jake shook off the man holding him, and Pierce's muscle ran like they had an army after them. The reporters didn't let up, going after the men like a pack of starving piranha. Within a minute, the plaza was empty.

"Are you INSANE!?" Jake was standing in the middle of the square, face red with anger.

"You told them about Pierce? About my father?"

"I was trying to save your life!" Amy said.

"What about my father's life? What do you think Pierce is going to do to him now that you outed him?" Jake yelled.

"Jake, I—"

"You do not get to make decisions for my family, Amy!"

"We can't just keep waiting," Amy said, her face hardening. "If we act, maybe we can force Pierce to make a mistake."

"And what if that mistake is killing my father? Do you even care?"

"Of course I care!"

Dan forced himself between Jake and Amy. "Guys! Hold on. Let's just calm down. We'll find your dad, Jake. I promise."

Jake glared at him. "And what if you don't? You going to stick up for her then, too, Dan? Those reporters were right about you. When are you going to get a mind of your own?"

Dan felt his own rage ignite. "Amy's doing her best!"

"For herself! Not for Atticus and me!"

"EVERYBODY SHUT UP!!"

Dan, Amy, and Jake wheeled on Atticus, their chests heaving. Atticus stood beneath a streetlight, Olivia's notebook open in his hands.

"Atticus," Jake said. "What? What is it?"

"I figured it out."

"Figured what out?"

Atticus took a deep breath, like he was steadying himself before going off a high dive.

"I know where Dad is," he said. "And I know where the silphium is, too."

CHAPTER 16

Atticus refused to say another word until they were deep in the stacks of the Tunis library, where Dr. Rosenbloom worked. It was still well before dawn, but the night security guard recognized Jake and Atticus and let them inside. Atticus guided them down narrow corridors of books that got older and older the farther they went. Every few seconds, Atticus stopped to examine a book, hauling a few into his increasingly heavy backpack.

Finally, they found themselves in a cramped reading room with an antique table and a few rickety chairs. Atticus pulled the books out of his pack and arranged them on the table, going through each one in turn.

Amy was standing across from Jake, but neither of them came close to looking at the other. They glowered at the dark table, their lingering anger filling the room like a black cloud. Dan felt suffocated by it and by Jake's words in the plaza. Amy was his sister. They always stuck together, no matter what. *And she did the right thing. Didn't she?*

"Att," Jake said. "Seriously. We don't have a lot of time here. If you know where they're keeping Dad—"

"No one's keeping Dad anywhere," Atticus said, his eyes meeting Jake's.

"What do you mean? Where is he?"

Atticus closed the book in front of him and took a deep breath. "This is going to sound crazy."

"Atticus, would you just—"

"Dad's in Atlantis."

Dan had never heard a silence as complete or as awkward as the one that followed Atticus's pronouncement. Everyone just sort of froze in place.

"Um . . . buddy," Dan said as delicately as possible, "I know we've all been under a little stress lately, but Atlantis doesn't, you know, um . . ."

"Exist," Jake said.

Atticus pushed his glasses up and turned to look at Amy. "Back in the medina, when you asked the man to let my father go, he acted like he didn't know what you were talking about, right?"

"These guys are well trained," she said. "They know how to lie when they need to."

"I know that," Atticus said. "But did you believe him?"

Amy stared down at the table, her brow wrinkling in concentration. "Yeah," she said. "I did."

"Me too," Atticus said. "In actuality, that's when it became clear."

"That your father is in Atlantis," Dan said. "Doing what, Att? Hanging out with the mermaids?"

Atticus ignored Dan and held up Olivia's notebook. "This is the page my dad was looking at before he left."

"Names and gibberish," Jake said. "We've been over this."

Atticus held up a finger. "But what if they're not gibberish? Look at the last sentence, the one that doesn't seem to make any sense. *The twentieth Hafsid claims to keep the testament of the failed strategoi.*"

Atticus opened a massive leather book marked *Caliphs of Ifriqiya*. Dan could almost see the wheels turning in his friend's head.

"The Hafsid was a dynasty that controlled Tunis, called Ifriqiya back then, from the thirteenth to sixteenth centuries. The twentieth Hafsid should mean the twentieth Caliph, or ruler. That was a man named Abu Umar Uthman ben Abul Hasan Muhammad. Uthman for short."

"Okay," Amy said. "So who's the failed *strategoi*?"

"That was a little harder," Atticus admitted. "A *strategoi* was a kind of general. The failed one could mean any number of them. But then I looked into those names from Plato's dialogues and found out that he based his character Hermocrates on a real guy."

"A general," Dan said, suddenly feeling the excitement that always built up inside of him when he saw Atticus at work.

"Exactly," Atticus said. "And apparently not a very good one. He was made a general but then had the title taken away because he didn't win enough battles."

"So . . ."

"So what Olivia is saying is that the twentieth Hafsid, Uthman, claimed to have the testament of the failed *strategoi*, Hermocrates. That testament must mean Plato's third dialogue, which was supposed to be named after him."

"Which you said doesn't exist," Jake said.

"It isn't *supposed* to exist." Atticus's eyes gleamed. "But what if it does?"

"So wait," Dan said. "What's this even have to do with Atlantis?"

"Nothing," Amy said. "Atticus, Dan is right, Atlantis is a myth."

"Everybody was pretty sure Troy was a myth," Jake said. "Until Calvert and Schliemann found it."

"But that's different!"

"How?" Atticus said, and then held up another book. "This is Plato's *Critias*, okay? It's the second of the three dialogues and the first time anyone in history mentions a place called Atlantis. It's *just* like how everyone thought Troy was something Homer made up in the *Iliad* until they actually found it."

"I don't know . . ." Amy said.

Atticus practically bounced in his chair. "Okay," he said. "Was there once an island-based world power with, like, super technology and mermaids that completely vanished? Duh, of course not! But could there have been some powerful kingdom thousands of years ago that was destroyed in a natural disaster? And then, over thousands of years, the myth of it grew until Plato wrote about it and called it Atlantis? Why not?"

"But we found Troy," Amy said. "With all the technology we have today, how could we have missed an entire *island*?"

"Who knows?" Atticus said. "If it's really, really, really old, maybe there's not a lot left to find. Or maybe we're looking in the wrong places. I mean, it's not like Plato left us a map in *Critias* or anything."

"But maybe he did in *Hermocrates*," Dan said.

"Exactly," Atticus said. "Look, all I know is that Atlantis theories have always been a kind of hobby for our dad. And the second he saw this stuff in Olivia's notebook, stuff that seemed to reference a way to find the *actual* Atlantis, he ran like his life depended on it."

Jake frowned. "You're saying he wasn't kidnapped at all."

"Exactly! He just saw one of the biggest discoveries in history and went after it. That's why his house was such a wreck. It wasn't ransacked. You know how Dad is! He was probably so excited to get after it that he tore the place apart grabbing what he needed and ran without even closing the door."

"Ran where, though?" Amy asked.

"To research Uthman, I'm guessing. If he can find where Uthman was keeping the *Hermocrates*, then maybe he can find Atlantis."

Amy considered a moment and then shook her head. "Atticus, you and Jake should go check on your dad, but Dan and I have to go back to searching for the silphium."

"Fine," Jake said. "Come on, Atticus. We can start at his house and go from there."

"Wait!" Atticus said as his brother reached for the door. "There's one more thing."

"What?"

Atticus sat back in his chair with his arms crossed over his chest and a broad smile on his face. He looked unusually pleased with himself.

"The note Olivia made about Leonardo's joke. Remember? When she asked him where she could find the silphium, he said she should look—"

"On the Island of the Athenian," Dan said. "But . . ."

The words had barely left Dan's mouth when it hit him like an avalanche.

"Plato," Dan said. "He was totally from Athens, wasn't he?"

"A born-and-raised Athenian," Atticus said, and waved his hands like he had just performed a magic trick. "Making Atlantis his island and where we'll find silphium."

Another astounded silence descended on the room. Dan felt as if his head was buzzing. Jake turned to Amy with a smirk.

"So," he said. "Looks like we're headed to the same place."

CHAPTER 17

Amy was on a ladder high above the library floor when her cell phone hummed. She set aside the book she was looking through and pulled it out.

Carthage Museum, read the text message.

Atticus and Jake had gone back to their father's to look for clues, while she and Dan stayed behind and researched Uthman and his reign. Looked like the others had hit on something first. Amy packed up the notes she had been taking and then slid down the ladder.

She went to the study room Dan had been in all morning, but her brother wasn't there. The table was covered with a clutter of books, papers, and candy wrappers. *Dan,* she thought. She could remember a time when his messiness drove her crazy but now . . .

Amy neatened the books and threw the wrappers away. She was about to put Dan's notes in his backpack when she saw a sheaf of brightly colored papers sticking out from it. Curious, Amy pulled one out.

It was a brochure advertising something called Bartleby's World-Famous Clown Academy. There was another for a baseball camp, and another for an astronaut camp. An application for the American School in Rome sat at the bottom. Each page was printed in bright jewel colors and covered with pictures of boys Dan's age. Boys running through parks or juggling torches. Boys sliding into home base.

Amy felt a dark hole open up inside her.

He's already making plans to leave.

She leafed through the brochures again. How long had Dan been hiding these? She'd tried to convince herself that his talk of leaving was a passing thing, but now . . . her last family member, the person she trusted most of all, had one foot out the door.

"Amy?"

Amy stuffed the brochures back into his pack and turned around.

"Everything okay?" Dan asked.

"Y-yeah," she stuttered, unable to meet his eyes. "Jake texted. They're at the Carthage Museum."

Amy pushed past Dan before he could say a word, nearly running into the hall outside. It was like the sheaf of papers stuffed inside his pack was a bomb, and she had to get away before it went off.

Amy stepped out of the gloom of the library, shielding her eyes from the Tunisian morning light. The buzzing sound of the call to prayer seemed to come from every direction at once. Everything seemed overloud and overbright. Dan appeared behind her and raised a hand out over the traffic until a cab skidded to a stop at the curb. Dan told the driver where they were going and the car pulled away from the library and joined the Tunisian traffic.

"Amy?" Dan asked. "You find anything helpful?"

She shook her head, eyes fixed out the window. "I just took some notes. Whatever seemed worthwhile."

They left the city traffic and moved onto a highway that spanned Lake Tunis. The glare of the sun on the steely water hit Amy's eyes like spikes and she had to look away.

Dan was sitting across from her with his arms wrapped around his backpack, holding it close to his chest as he looked out the window. A corner of bright blue paper stuck out the top of the pack. She wanted to say something to Dan, but what? *Don't go? How could you?* For the first time, there was something between them too immense for words. *He's really going to do it. He's really going to leave.* Amy couldn't breathe.

The rest of the trip passed in a blur. The cab lurched to a stop and Dan piled out and headed up the side-walk to the museum, his backpack bouncing on his shoulder. Jake and Atticus were waiting. Everything suddenly snapped back into focus. They had work to do. Amy shook herself and paid the driver.

"What have you got?" she asked when she joined them at the museum's entrance.

"We found this in Dad's living room," Atticus said, handing over a scrap of paper. "When we thought he had been kidnapped, we figured all the mess was just

Pierce's goons ransacking the place, so we missed this."

Amy unfolded the piece of paper. "Dr. Abdallah, two P.M."

"He's a researcher here," Jake said. "We called and told him we were coming."

Jake pulled open the glass door to the museum and they were met by an elegant Tunisian man in the lobby.

"Jake! Atticus! I've heard so much about you both. Everyone here was terribly worried to hear you don't know your father's whereabouts."

"Thank you, Dr. Abdallah," Jake said. "We think you were our father's last appointment before we lost track of him."

Dr. Abdallah signaled the receptionist, who buzzed them through into a long hallway lined with offices.

"Of course," the doctor said as he led them down the hall. "But we didn't talk for more than a few moments. Your father seemed . . . agitated. Excited! More excited than I've ever seen him, in fact."

"What did he say?"

"We will soon be exhibiting a large collection of fifteenth-century artifacts," Dr. Abdallah said as he unlocked a heavy door at the end of the hall. "He wanted an early look at the collection."

"Can we see it as well?" Atticus asked. "We'll be very careful."

Dr. Abdallah showed them into a large room full of tables covered in artifacts and stacks of old books.

"Does anything relate to Uthman?" Jake asked.

"Ah, like father like son!" Dr. Abdallah smiled. "Dr. Rosenbloom asked the same thing. Right over here."

Dr. Abdallah showed them to a back corner of the room, to a table displaying clay vases and gleaming metalwork. Atticus went immediately to a small stack of books and opened the first one.

"There are English translations to the side," Dr. Abdallah said. "I will be in my office if you need me."

As the doctor left the room, Atticus leaned into one of the translations like he was trying to dive in.

"What's it say, Att?" Dan asked.

Atticus ignored him and read, flipping pages, his face getting closer and closer to the book. "Aw, man!"

"What is it?" Jake asked.

Atticus turned another page and shook his head. "This doesn't make sense!"

"What?" Jake asked.

"Well, it's sort of a diary," Atticus said. "Uthman's talking about meeting a traveling merchant who claimed to possess a copy of *Hermocrates*. It sounds like Uthman wasn't a hundred percent sure the guy was legit, but he says the book went into more detail about Atlantis. All about its history and culture, but nothing about where it actually *was*. All he says is that in older times, it was called by another name."

"What other name?"

Atticus turned the page and found a footnote passage. "Tartessos."

"Tartessos?" Dan said. "Never heard of it."

"Me either." Jake frowned.

Dan sighed, frustrated. "Okay, I guess we'll look at old maps and try to find an island called Tartessos."

"Wait!" Amy tore through her notebook, running her finger along each page.

"What is it, Amy? You have something?"

She dropped the notebook on the table and riffled through the pages.

"It was here," she mumbled. "Right here."

"What was?" Dan asked.

Amy turned the pages until she came to a map. A notation below indicated that it depicted the world as it was in the fourth century B.C.

"It's not really the right century, but I thought it was interesting and wanted a copy."

Amy stabbed her finger at the coastline of what was now Tunisia, then drew it west past Morocco and across the Strait of Gibraltar. To the north lay the borders of a country they all recognized as Spain.

Just inland from the southwest coast, there was a large region marked with a circle. In that circle was written a single word:

Tartessos.

"Ladies and gentlemen," Dan said, breaking the silence. "It looks like we have just discovered Atlantis."

"Awesomesauce!" said Atticus, and pumped his fist.

CHAPTER 18

April May wondered how to bill her clients in a way that really captured the scale of the work she did. Not by the hour or per project, but by the empty two liter of Electroshock Cherry Limeade Caffeine Blast. One glass consumed meant an amateur job—breaking into a gmail or Facebook account. Breaking into the Cahills' systems had been a three-bottle project and she would charge handsomely for it.

And now here she was sitting in front of her two gleaming monitors, surrounded by *six* empty bottles. A seventh was in her hand and half empty already.

Finding out what J. Rutherford Pierce was up to was the biggest project of her career. Part of the problem was that before a certain time, there barely *was* a J. Rutherford Pierce. Oh, he existed, but hardly in the form he was now. He was a second rater, a loser.

How did he become the man he was? And more important, what kind of man is he planning on becoming next?

It had seemed so innocent in the beginning when he hired her to get some dirt on a couple of rich brats.

Easy. Harmless. But then she saw the *picture.* Some thick-necked goon holding the business end of a hypodermic needle to Amy Cahill's neck. Pierce didn't want to embarrass Amy, he wanted to *kill* her. And probably her friends, too.

April May tried to tell herself it was a mistake. A muscleman who jumped the gun and went in for an unsanctioned kill. It worked for a while as a reasonable theory, but the more April May learned, the more it sounded like something else — wishful thinking. She needed to know for sure. And if a man like Pierce *was* trying to kill a couple of kids, what was the endgame?

April May put her fingers to the keyboard and soon that delicious feeling of becoming one with the networks washed over her. She avoided all of the obvious places information might be. Pierce's e-mail. His cell phone. He was too smart to store anything important somewhere so obvious. No, anything worthwhile would be on the Founders Media network, hidden away on a remote hub. Since she had built a great deal of the security protocols for Founders, she was going to get past them. It was just a matter of time.

April May slithered through human resources and accounting, then dipped in and out of a few isolated terminals. She searched the hard drive of a reporter in Bogotá, Colombia, and the Twitter account of a Founders Media intern in Des Moines, Iowa. April found a few juicy secrets here and there — some even worth filing away for later—but nothing that explained what Pierce was up to.

There was a *ping* as April moved through the system. She ignored it at first but the sound grew louder each time, and finally she forced herself to break the trance and look over at her second monitor.

There, in pale green letters, were the words: *There's a mouse in the maze.*

April May almost spilled her Electroshock Cherry Limeade. *Interesting.*

An old security subroutine had been activated. She had created it to watch for invaders on the network, and it looked like it had just sniffed someone out. April May delved into the system logs. This particular mouse had been poking around for a few days now, but the strange thing was, it hadn't done any damage. No viruses. No downloads of sensitive data. That eliminated blackmail, corporate espionage, and most black hat hackers.

"Who are you?" she asked the little mouse.

April May turned her attention to the second monitor. She tracked the mouse for a few minutes, a funny feeling growing in her stomach. The mouse was very good and *very* familiar. A few minutes later, and she was positive. She was staring at the Cahills' very own pet hacker.

April May smiled. The mouse was good, nearly as good as she was. She took another slug of soda and inspiration struck. Searching Pierce's systems could take weeks and might not work. But sitting right in front of her was one of the Cahill team. Did *the Cahills* know why they were targets?

"Stay right there," she said, staring at the screen. "Stay right where you are."

April spent the next hour building elaborate security protocols, all the while keeping an eye on her mouse. Once she was satisfied, she opened the chat interface. She was about to start typing but stopped herself. *No reason to miss an opportunity.* April May wove a very clever and nearly invisible bit of code into the chat system. The mouse would see nothing but text, but if it responded, she would get a tiny foothold into the new Cahill system. Once she was done, April May cracked her knuckles and set them on the keys.

What do I say?

She felt a strange bundle of nerves in her stomach as she thought of the real live human behind the lights of her system. She paused, then lowered a single finger and typed two words.

Pony sat in front of his computer, staring at two words in glowing type.

Hi there.

He looked behind him, expecting to see Ian or one of the others messing with him, but the command center was empty. Just him, the darkness, and the words. He set his fingers on the keys and then pulled them back again. This was strange. Too strange to not be careful. He moved to his second machine and did some tracing.

"Unbelievable," he whispered. "Un-freaking-believable!"

He had never seen such a complicated routing. And so masterfully done! The signal was coming from outside the command center but it was impossible to tell from where. Whoever was contacting him could be in the house next door or at a cyber café in Mumbai.

The *really* interesting thing, though, was that the routing was almost too complicated. There was no reason to go that overboard unless you were trying to send a message. But what message?

Who do you know that's this good? And to that question there was only one answer. April May.

Pony scrambled for his phone. Someone had to tell him what to do! He called Ian, and then Hamilton and Jonah, but got no response. *It's four* A.M.*! Who goes to bed this early!?* He was about to run downstairs, but a thought checked him. What if she was gone when he got back?

Apparently, this one was up to him. Pony checked the communication stream again. Definitely nothing coming through but plain text. April May wasn't sending a virus or anything like that. She only wanted to talk. Pony decided to keep his response simple, too.

Hi.

His reply sat on screen for a moment. He started to

think that maybe April May had gotten spooked, but there was another *ping*.

You know who I am?

Sure, Pony typed. *You're the Queen of the Universe.*

Flattering, April responded. *Wanna fill me in on you?*

They call me Pony.

You're not bad.

Pony grinned. He was really doing it! He was talking to the great April May! He was afraid his brain was going to rupture from pure fanboy glee. His fingers shook as he resumed typing.

What can I do for you? Pony typed.

Something's been bothering me lately, April typed. *Thought you might have an opinion about it.*

Pony frowned.

I won't give you anything that will hurt my friends.

I'm not asking for any, April May replied. *I'm just asking a question. Freelance genius to freelance genius.*

Pony flushed with pride, but thought a moment before he answered. *What do you want to know?*

April May stared at the words on the screen, a jolt of nerves in her stomach. She grabbed her bottle of soda and drowned it in caffeine. The *ping* of an e-mail notification came from her secondary system.

April glanced up. One e-mail stood out from the

others, bold and highlighted in red, like it was screaming at her. It was from Pierce, demanding to know
where the Cahills were. What they were doing. How
he could find them. April took a swig of Electroshock
Cherry Limeade Caffeine Blast and began to type.

Who's the bad guy? You? Or me?

CHAPTER 19

"But how can Atlantis be Spain?" Dan asked as the Mediterranean slipped beneath their small plane. "Last time I checked, Spain wasn't even an island!"

Atticus was sitting in the back, wedged between Amy and Jake, his lap full of books. He had been immersed in his research ever since they left the museum. After their chase through the streets of Tunis, there was far too much media and police interest in the Cahills for them to go to the airport, so Jonah's pilot had made a last-minute switch-up. The four kids had rented a boat and met the pilot and his seaplane a mile offshore. It would be another hour still before they landed near the Spanish coast and were picked up by another boat.

"In actuality, it matches up pretty well with what Plato wrote," Atticus said. "Atlantis was supposed to be to the west of the Pillars of Hercules, which we know are the rocks on either side of the Strait of Gibraltar. Spain is definitely west of that. And apparently Plato's not the only one who thinks this is the place. A scientist named Richard Freund has been studying the possibility for years."

"So why haven't we heard about him?" Dan asked.

Atticus shifted in his seat. "Well . . . most people think he's nuts."

"Sounds like our kind of guy."

"But he's found some interesting stuff," Atticus said. "According to him, there used to be a huge bay in southern Spain. He says Atlantis was built right on the water in a series of concentric circles with amazing temples and ports and everything. And what we know about Tartessos definitely matches up with the legend of Atlantis. It was incredibly rich, largely from the ores it mined from the surrounding area. But then, thousands of years ago, a massive tsunami swept into that area and would have wrecked the entire city. Over the years, it was covered with dozens of feet of silt. Eventually, the whole thing became a big marshland and Spain made it a national park."

"So does this guy have actual, you know, proof?" Dan asked.

Atticus's voice got high and squeaky. "He has some interesting images on ground-penetrating radar," he said carefully. "And some people agree that some sites look like they could, maybe, be memorials to the lost city. There's *something* down there all right, but the whole area is too marshy to do a lot of excavating. I don't know! It's why we're checking it out, okay?" Atticus plunged back into his books.

Dan looked around the plane, frowning. He and Amy had flown all around the world, a lot of the time with Atticus and Jake with them. But he'd never known a flight so silent. Amy stared out the plane's window with the same broody silence that had surrounded her since they had left the library.

Dan knew what it was about, but there was nothing he could say. As slick as she'd tried to be, he'd seen her looking in his backpack. He knew what she must have found.

Dan flushed. He couldn't help feeling as if he'd been caught doing something shameful, like stealing or conspiring with the enemy. But they were just some brochures. And he'd told Amy that he was done with the Cahills after they figured out how to stop Pierce. *If* they figured out how to stop Pierce. He couldn't do this anymore. It felt as if his skin was getting tighter every day, until soon it would suffocate him. Is that what she wanted for him?

The more he thought about it, the more his guilt was replaced with anger. Anger at *Amy*. He'd been mad at her before—a lot—but it was usually a "hey you borrowed my hoodie without asking" kind of anger. This was real, burning hot, even teary. So much so that he couldn't bring himself to say anything about it. They'd been through so much together and they'd always been able to talk through anything. It was the only way they'd survived. It was impossible, unthinkable, but something had changed.

The pilot announced that he was preparing to land. Dan clipped his seat belt in place and looked out the window, gulping when all he saw below them was the iron sweep of the ocean. Landing without a runway just didn't seem right.

It ended up being surprisingly smooth, though, and minutes later they were met by a fishing boat. They all stepped uneasily onto the plane's pontoons before taking the hand of a grizzled-looking fisherman and crossing over onto the boat deck.

Dan steadied himself against the railing as Jake helped Atticus with his life vest. Amy stood off by herself, again, the hood of her sweatshirt pulled up as she watched the churn of the boat's wake with empty eyes. *This is ridiculous!* Dan started to cross the deck toward her, but something stopped him.

Once we have the silphium, we'll both be more relaxed, Dan thought. *We'll talk then.* Dan huddled against the railing, hoping it was true.

A Land Rover met them at the shore and brought them into Doñana National Park, which did not look to Dan like the home of the world's most famous sunken city. It was a mix of sand dunes and lush, reedy marshlands. About five miles inland, they moved onto a flat plain of sun-bleached dirt dotted with sprigs of dry reeds and tufts of grass.

"So, this is Atlantis," Dan said. "Man, the Aquaman comic books were *way* off."

"You wouldn't look so great, either, if you'd been covered in silt for a few thousand years," Atticus shot back.

A dusty camp came into view. It consisted of a handful of tents with scientists bustling around in khaki and hiking boots. Their Land Rover came to a halt just outside of camp.

"What if we're wrong," Atticus said, looking even younger than usual. "What if Dad's not here and Pierce really does have him?"

Dan looked back at his friend. "Hey, when are you *ever* wrong? He's here. So, what's the plan? Jake, do you want to —"

Amy threw open her door and started across the plain. Dan and the others exchanged a look.

It's like we're not even here, Dan thought, and then the three of them piled out of the car with Jake in the lead.

"Hey!" Jake called after Amy. "You remember that whole thing about my dad disliking you, right?"

"Yes," said Amy, not even bothering to turn around. "And I also remember you saying that Dan and I should try making a direct appeal. Just hang back and let me talk to him."

Dan could see the tension in Jake's shoulders ahead of him.

"All due respect to your Leader-tude," Jake called, "but he's my dad and you don't exactly seem in the most diplomatic frame of mind right now."

"I'm fine!"

"You're acting like a crazy person!" Jake fired back.

"Dad!" yelled Atticus, and ran past everyone into the camp.

Dr. Rosenbloom had just emerged from one of the tents. Atticus threw his arms around his very startled father, who spun him around.

"What's going on?" Dr. Rosenbloom asked. "Att, what are you doing here? Are you okay?"

"We're fine."

Jake glanced at Amy and then ran over to join Atticus. "We saw your house," Jake said. "We thought something might have happened to you."

Dr. Rosenbloom's expression cleared and he laughed. "Ah, I guess I was in a bit of a hurry. Sorry if it worried you guys. But aren't you supposed to be back in Rome? Did you miss your flight?" Dr. Rosenbloom waved his own question away. "You know what? It doesn't matter! When you guys see what we've found here, your heads are going to explode right off your shoulders. Come on, let me show you!"

Amy stepped forward, and Dan put up a hand to hold her back. "Amy, wait. Let them—"

"Dr. Rosenbloom!" Amy called.

Dr. Rosenbloom turned. His smile evaporated the second he laid eyes on her. The glow that lit his face from the moment he saw his sons disappeared instantly, replaced with something dark and cold.

"Dad —" Atticus began.

"So, you were worried about me?" Dr. Rosenbloom repeated, anger coloring his voice.

"It's true," Jake said. "We —"

Dr. Rosenbloom broke away from them and marched across the field, his eyes locked on Amy.

"Sir, I . . ."

"We may be out in the middle of nowhere, Ms. Cahill, but we do get the news," he said. "If you think for a single second that I'm going to let my sons get involved with a pair of entitled brats like you and your brother, then you're out of your mind! I won't let you do to Jake what you did to that Tolliver boy!"

"Dad!" Jake exclaimed as Amy's face went totally white.

"Not another word, Jake," Dr. Rosenbloom snapped. "Take your brother into my tent right now."

"Amy didn't do anything!" Jake protested. "Those news reports are lies!"

Dr. Rosenbloom whirled on his son. "That boy's parents were lying, then? Is that what you're saying? Is that what she told you?"

"No! It's just — Amy and Evan were trying to do something very important and he got hurt, but it wasn't Amy's fault. She tried to keep him from getting involved. She'd never let anyone get hurt if she could help it."

"I said, not another word!"

"Sir, please," Amy cut in. "Dan and I will go. Right now. I promise. You'll never see us again. But I need to know about silphium. It's very important. Have you found any?"

Dr. Rosenbloom walked over, not stopping until he nearly ran her down. He glared at her with a heat that made Dan flinch.

"We found two sealed jars this morning," Dr. Rosenbloom said through clenched teeth. "They had markings that indicated silphium seeds were inside."

"Can we see them?" Dan asked, trying to move between Amy and Jake and Atticus's dad. "Like my sister said. It's incredibly important."

Dr. Rosenbloom shook his head. "I wouldn't dream of it. And anyway, you're too late. I sent them on already."

"Where?" Amy persisted.

"One went to colleagues in Tunis for study. The other's on its way to the Global Seed Vault in Svalbard. Both places are out of your reach. And now? I believe you were going?"

Svalbard? Dan thought, and looked to Atticus.

"It's a vault built into the side of a mountain in the Arctic Circle," Atticus said. "They're using it to store seeds from all over the world."

"And the vault is shut tight, so there's no thrill-seeking to be done there," Dr. Rosenbloom said, nearly shaking with rage. "They only have staff at the vault a couple of times a year. They're waiting to store the silphium and then they're headed out."

"Thank you, sir," Amy said. She kept her head raised, but Dan could see that she couldn't quite look

Dr. Rosenbloom in the eye. She turned to Jake and Atticus. "You two stay with your father. Dan and I will take it from here."

Amy turned her back on them and started to walk away. Her back was straight, but they could all see how badly she was trembling.

"Amy! Wait!" said Jake as he charged after her.

Dr. Rosenbloom reached out and caught his son as Jake tried to rush past him. "This is over," he said, grabbing Jake's shirt and shaking him for emphasis. "You and Atticus are going back to school, and I'm calling the Tunisian police right now."

Jake tore out of his father's grip. "Then you'll be calling them on me, too."

"Jake!"

"I can't explain everything now," he said. "I just need you to trust me. Amy and Dan haven't *made* us do anything. We're doing this because we know how important it is. It's probably the most important thing Atticus or I will ever do. We'll be careful, I swear. But we're going. Now."

"Jake, don't you dare—"

Jake's face was granite as he turned away from his father. Dr. Rosenbloom stepped forward to grab Jake again, and Atticus ran out behind him. Amy stood motionless near the Land Rover, watching the Rosenblooms sprint toward her, with what looked like tears glistening in the corners of her eyes. When she saw Dan looking, she wiped them away and fixed her eyes on the ground.

"Atticus!" Dr. Rosenbloom cried as his sons streaked toward the car. He looked shocked, as if he had woken up into an alternate universe.

"Guys," Amy said, putting herself between Jake and Atticus and the car. "You can't—"

"It doesn't matter what you say, either," Jake said. "We're not doing this for you. We're doing it because it's right. So unless *both* you and Dan want us gone, we're coming with you."

Amy turned to Dan, who was sitting in the front seat of the car. The force of her expectation was like a punch to his chest. He looked from her to Jake and Atticus.

"We need them, Amy," Dan said. "They're coming with us."

"Stop!" Dr. Rosenbloom shouted as he ran toward the Land Rover. Jake and Atticus jumped in, and then Dan grabbed his sister and pulled her into the car.

"Let's go," he shouted to the driver. "And hurry!"

Dan glanced back at Amy as they took off in a cloud of dust. Her eyes were filled with the same emotion he'd seen back at the library. A look that screamed out that she'd been betrayed, and by the person she trusted the most.

Dan made himself look away.

"We'll be in Tunis in a few hours," he announced to the group. "We need a plan. Thoughts, everybody?"

Amy was frozen in place, shocked breathless. What had happened to the two of them? Dan looked at her lately as if she were a stranger, but he had to know she was only trying to keep everyone safe. Didn't he?

Amy drew herself over the backseat and into the rear of the Land Rover's storage compartment. She leaned over their backpacks so it looked like she was checking their gear, and pulled out her phone. She dialed, and while it rang she kept her eyes locked on Dan and Jake and Atticus, her heart aching to see them making plans without her.

The ringing stopped and their pilot answered.

"It's me," Amy whispered. "Yes. But I'll need you to bring some things with you when you come."

Amy rattled off a list and then she looked ahead. The boys still were absorbed in their plans. Dan and Jake and Atticus seemed so far away, almost as if the inside of the car had been split into two separate worlds. Something cold clicked into place.

And that's the safest place for them, she thought. *Far away. The way it always should have been.*

The pilot asked her a question, snapping Amy back to reality.

"No," she said, answering him. "There's been a change of plans. Listen up. . . ."

CHAPTER 20

Nellie hid in the bathroom, listening as the last of the late-shift employees filed out of their labs. A half hour after their voices faded, the cleaning crews moved in with the swish of mops and the whine of vacuums. Finally, the only thing Nellie could hear was the soft ticking of the air conditioners winding down for the night.

Nellie took a breath, then unfolded herself from her perch on top of the toilet bowl.

Outside the bathroom, the corridor was filled with a mix of safety lights and deep shadows. Nellie glanced up at the security cameras mounted along the ceiling. They were stationary, and she was pretty sure she could stay out of their fields of view.

She slinked up the stairs to the next floor, opening and closing doors with excruciating care so they didn't make a sound. She made it to the fourth floor, then consulted her mental map. The entrance to the secret staircase was supposed to be at a dead end — left, then right, then left again from where she was standing.

Nellie started down the first hall, but dove back into the shadows at the click of a door ahead of her. She flattened against a wall as a small woman in a white lab coat stepped into the corridor and walked down the hall. The woman patted at her pockets, growing increasingly frustrated as she searched for something. Once the woman was out of sight, Nellie waited and listened before continuing on. Every step confirmed that she and the woman were headed in the same direction.

Maybe she knows I'm behind her and is leading me into a trap. Maybe this ends with me in the hands of a couple of goons like the ones that nearly killed the kiddos.

Nellie shook off the unproductive thoughts and made herself continue forward. Her legs weren't quite steady. Left, then right, then left again. Nellie hung back in the dark and peeked around a corner. The woman was at the end of a hall with her back to Nellie. She was still digging through her pockets, muttering to herself. Nellie heard a clink of change and then a deep *ka-chunk*. The woman moved aside and Nellie caught sight of what was at the end of the hall.

It wasn't a secret entrance.

It was a vending machine.

The scientist reached into a slot for her snack, tore open the bag, and chowed down an entire bag of honey BBQ pork rinds, going so far as to upend the bag so she could suck back the last remaining crumbs.

Hmm. Maybe she isn't a part of an international criminal conspiracy, after all.

Nellie flattened herself into the shadows once again as the woman moved past her. When Madame Pork Rinds was gone, Nellie tiptoed down to the vending machine, running her hands along the walls, searching for a seam or a hollow place that might indicate an entrance. There was nothing.

The vending machine itself looked perfectly normal. Glass front and black metal sides. A slot for change and a place to swipe credit cards. Next to the card reader there was a large red A surrounded in white. The machine itself was full of candy and chips and rolls of mints. Nellie nudged it with one hand but it didn't move. She set her shoulder into it and pushed, still nothing.

"Come on, you stupid thing. I know there's more than pork rinds in you! There has to be!"

Nellie gave it another push, and when it gave nothing in return, her frustration hit a breaking point. She kicked at the thing and pushed, rocking it back and forth.

"Open up! Open up, you stupid thing! Open sesame!"

"Hey!"

Nellie gasped and whirled. She was face-to-face with a man in a charcoal-gray suit who was built to more or less the exact same specifications as the vending machine. A radio receiver sat in one ear and Nellie spied a gun-shaped bulge underneath his jacket.

Nellie's back was against the machine, and she could only look on in horror as the man strode toward her, reaching into his jacket.

"Wait, no, I was just—"

The guard pulled out a handful of change. "You scientists are all the same," he said with a shake of his head. "So excitable. You have to love your machines if you want to get anything out of them. Treat 'em nice."

He turned to Nellie with an odd smile on his chiseled face.

"So? What is it that you wanted, Doc?"

Nellie opened her mouth to answer, but words fled when she caught sight of the ID card hanging from the man's belt. It was white, just like hers, but instead of the blue D as on her card, his sported a bright red A.

Nellie glanced back at the A on the vending machine. It was a perfect match for the one on the guard's ID. A volley of fireworks went off in Nellie's head.

"Uh, ma'am?"

"Pork rinds," Nellie said with a smile. "I'll have the pork rinds."

CHAPTER 21

Amy stood alone on deck late that night, looking up at glistening stars surrounded by black. They were in the open ocean, somewhere between the coasts of Spain and Morocco. There wasn't a trace of land or a gleam of artificial light in any direction. Amy thought the view must have been no different than the one seen by the sailors of Carthage or Atlantis.

She climbed the stairs up onto the bridge. Everyone else was down below. Amy had explained that due to a delay in getting fuel, the plane wouldn't meet them for hours yet, so everyone should get some rest.

Amy knelt beside the boat's big steering wheel and took the key from the ignition beneath it. She dropped it into her palm where it joined the spare she had found among the captain's things. The keys clinked together in her palm, catching the moonlight. She walked to the railing and turned her hand over. The keys fell into the water, hitting with a barely audible *plop*. There was a flash of silver in the moonlight and then they were swallowed up by the dark.

"What are you doing?"

Amy turned. Jake was standing at the hatch that led down to the crew compartment.

"I was just . . . getting some air."

Jake climbed up to the bridge, where he leaned against the railing and looked out onto the sea. The water was flat but for a few low, rolling swells, banded with slivers of moonlight.

"You should go get some sleep," Amy said nervously. "The plane will be here in a few hours."

Jake nodded, but kept staring out into the dark water. "Do you think they knew it was coming?"

The sudden shift threw Amy. "Who? Did they know what was coming?"

"The people in Atlantis," he said. "Or Tartessos. Or whatever it was called. Atticus said it was probably one of the greatest cities of all time. I was thinking since they had accomplished so much, maybe they couldn't imagine the end coming. I bet that's what killed them." Jake looked back over his shoulder at Amy. "Thinking they were invincible."

"Jake . . ."

"It used to be that I knew what you were going to do or what Dan was going to do almost before you did it. We were that in sync. But now it seems like all any of us do is fight. I don't like what I see coming, Amy."

An impulse to contradict him flared in Amy, but it burned itself out before she could give it voice. "I know," she said. It was barely a whisper.

Jake took a step toward her just as the distant whine of engines broke the silence. Jake looked up as the seaplane's running lights winked into view. Moonlight glinted off of its wings as it angled in for a landing.

"I guess he's early," Jake said. "We can talk about this later. I'll go get the others."

He started to go but Amy grabbed his sleeve to hold him back. "What are you—?"

"I'm going to Svalbard," she said. "Alone."

"What? Amy—"

"Everyone will be waiting for us in Tunis," she said. "Reporters, police, Pierce's men. Svalbard is the only chance."

"Fine, but going alone is crazy! Dad said the place will be empty and locked up. You'll never get in alone. Together we could—"

"I'm not letting anyone else get hurt over this," Amy said. "You're right, Jake. We're not invincible. And Pierce is too good. He's too smart."

There was a roar of engines and then a splash as the seaplane landed. Jake took hold of Amy's arm as she turned toward the boat's railing.

"You're right," he said. "Leave Dan and Atticus behind. But let me come with you."

The expression on Jake's face nearly sent Amy to her knees. Despite everything, all the fights and the hurt, Jake wouldn't hesitate to put himself in danger to help her. She knew exactly how he felt, because she felt the same. Amy felt something bright flare up inside of her.

But the brief rush of joy couldn't withstand the cold wall of fear, worry, and guilt she'd built up. She knew what she had to do. Amy thought of her grandmother, imagined the spine of steel that ran through Grace, and forced herself to look Jake in the eye.

"I don't love you," she said. "I know you think I do. You think that there's this . . . thing between us, but there isn't. There never was, and there never will be."

There was a pause, and then the light in Jake's eyes began to slowly fade. Amy was gutted to see it go, but she couldn't look away. She couldn't let up. Jake's grip on her arm loosened. The plane taxied to a stop fifty feet from the boat and the pilot popped the rear door.

"I've disabled the boat," Amy said. "But there's plenty of food and water on board. You'll all be safe until I send someone for you. If something happens to me, tell Dan to gather what we have on Pierce and call the FBI."

Before Jake could protest, Amy grabbed her pack and dove off the side of the boat. The chilly water hit her like a fist but she was up and pulling herself through the low swells in seconds. She could hear shouting behind her now. The plane was thirty feet away, then twenty, then ten.

The pilot reached down and took her by the wrist, pulling her up onto the wide pontoon. He wrapped a towel around her as she stepped up into the plane. Amy turned to shut the door.

"AMY!"

Dan was on deck now, standing just behind Jake. Her brother screamed her name and Amy felt hot tears filling her eyes.

"AMY!"

The plane's engines spun up and the propeller began to turn. Dan stripped off his shoes and shirt and dove off the boat. He disappeared in the black, and seconds later she saw his thin white arms tearing through the water. The pilot turned back to her.

"What do I do?"

"Go. Now!" Amy said as Dan got closer and closer. In another few strokes he'd be able to grab the pontoons.

"But there's someone in the water," the pilot called out over the engines. "Shouldn't we—"

"Just go!"

Amy slammed the door and fell into her seat. Amy could hear Jake, Atticus, and Dan yelling, even over the noise of the propellers. Each shout was like a fist digging into her, clutching at her insides. Amy closed her eyes tight and the engines surged, drowning the boys out. The plane began to pull away, picking up speed. There was a sluice of water below and then the strangely heavy feeling as they strained into the sky.

Amy opened her eyes. Below, the boat grew smaller until Dan and the others faded into the distance. Soon, the boat was nothing but a white dot amid the black.

Amy made herself look straight ahead, staring out the pilot's window, as they soared away into the darkness.

Nellie felt herself grow tense as she passed rooms of patients hooked up to pinging machinery and wheezy breathing machines. She had been promising herself for days that she'd come to see Fiske and had been avoiding it, telling herself that the Trilon investigation was too important. But finally the excuses didn't hold anymore. It wasn't that she didn't love Fiske, it's just that she hated hospitals. Even when they were as luxe as the Callender Institute, they still creeped her out.

She had been twelve when her grandma got cancer, and Nellie had never quite gotten over seeing her laid up in the stark white of that room. As if being sick wasn't bad enough, Nellie's grandma had to do it while being assaulted by fluorescent lighting and the nose-stinging smell of disinfectant. It seemed like the ultimate insult. And the food! Hospitals should be about love and healing and comfort, about beef stew seasoned with just the right amount of thyme and rosemary. Instead, her grandma got mystery meat and iceberg lettuce. Dessert was a sad little cube of green Jell-O.

How was someone supposed to embrace life eating that garbage? Why would they want to?

Well, it won't be like that for Fiske, Nellie thought, swinging the wicker picnic basket she had brought with her. She had waited too long to visit, but she was going to make up for it now. *I'm going to heal that man!*

"Nellie Gomez!" Fiske practically leaped out of bed as she stepped into his room.

"Fiske!"

Nellie tried to hide her shock at seeing him. The report she had gotten from the kiddos was that Fiske was as gray as dishwater and wrinklier than a man ten years his senior. That certainly wasn't the case now. Fiske practically glowed. His skin was smooth and ruddy, his eyes bright.

"You look amazing!"

Fiske laughed, loud and hearty. "As do you, as always. Is that a care package I see in your hands?"

"It is, but I think I should go find someone who's actually sick and give it to them!"

"If it gets me some of your delicious cooking, I will endeavor to be appropriately moribund. Now, bring it here, Nellie! Bring it here!"

Fiske rubbed his palms together with the eagerness of a little kid as Nellie set the basket down and threw it open. "Okay," she said, pulling out stacks of plastic tubs. "We have a big bowl of chicken and dumpling soup followed by an apple cider–brined pork chop, rice pilaf, mixed green salad, and for dessert . . ."

Nellie whipped the top off a tub.

"Banoffee pie!"

"Banoffee pie!" Fiske exclaimed. "My favorite! I barely know where to start."

Nellie handed him a big silver spoon. "Chicken soup," she said.

"With pleasure!"

Nellie found a seat next to the bed, smiling as Fiske dug in with obvious relish.

"Delicious," he said through stuffed mouthfuls. "Marvelous. Now tell me the news. How are Dan and Amy? How is the hunt!?"

Fiske polished off the soup and moved on to the pork chop, not even bothering with a knife and fork. He picked it up in his hands and tore into it with his teeth.

"Uh . . . they're fine," Nellie said, distracted by the spectacle of Fiske eating like a hungry tiger. "They found the whiskers and are in Tunis now searching for the silphium. I think Amy is feeling the stress, though. She sent most of the team back to the States."

"Excellent!" Fiske said. "Excellent."

"Excellent? Why is—"

"Amy is feeling her power, Nellie. Her mastery. She is coming into her own. When a person does that, other people can start to feel like . . . how can I say it? Like anchors rather than sails. Do you catch my meaning? My word, this pork chop is delicious!"

"Fiske, are you sure you're okay? You seem—"

"My dear girl, I haven't felt this good since I was

sixteen," he said. "No! Scratch that. Even then I didn't feel this strong, this fast, this . . . attuned. I'm seeing things I've never seen before. The world is as clear to me as a pane of freshly washed glass."

Nellie reached for the phone by Fiske's bedside. "You know, maybe I should talk to your doc—OW!"

Fiske's hand shot out of nowhere and clamped down on Nellie's wrist. She cried out as her bones bowed under the pressure, ready to snap.

"Fiske, you're hurting me!"

He yanked his hand back like he had been shocked. His mouth fell open and his eyes went cold and hollow. His shoulders fell. Suddenly, his hand that had the strength of a steel vise the second before was as weak as a kitten's paw.

"Oh, Nellie. Oh, Nellie. I'm so sorry. No!"

Tears began to fill Fiske's eyes. They coursed down his cheeks as he drew into himself like a piece of paper being slowly crumpled.

"I'm so sorry. I don't . . . I don't know what happened. It's like I don't know my own strength. I act before I even think. What's happening to me?"

Nellie pushed the lunch basket out of the way and laid a comforting hand on Fiske's shoulder. His face was beet red, his features scrunched together. He looked like a bewildered child.

"It's okay," she said quietly, stroking his arm. "You're going to be fine. We're just going to talk to your doctor. Okay?"

Fiske seized on the idea like a life rope. "Yes!" he said. "Talk to Dr. Callender. He always knows what to—"

Before he could finish his sentence, Fiske's eyes fell shut and his breath evened out. He was asleep, his arms crossed over his chest, clutching himself tight. The hand just beneath his chin was shaking visibly.

Nellie tore out of the room toward a nurses' station just outside. The nurse's eyes went wide as Nellie strode toward her.

"Hey! You! I want to see Dr. Jeffrey Callender. Right now!"

Nellie stood outside Dr. Callender's office, tapping her foot impatiently while he sat at his desk speaking with a young woman in a bright red blazer. Fiske had been one of the strongest, most in-control men she had ever known. When the kiddos went to see him, they said he looked tired and weak but they didn't say anything about a reaction like this.

"Ms. Gomez?"

Nellie looked up as Dr. Callender waved her inside. The woman in the red blazer jostled Nellie on her way to the door.

"Hey!" Nellie said.

The woman in red didn't say a word. She already had a cell phone stuck to her ear and was chatting away as she walked.

"Some people say excuse me!" Nellie called.

The woman didn't even turn her head. Nellie rolled her eyes and was about to go in the office when she saw something familiar hanging off the back of the woman's purse — a white key card imprinted with a large red A. Beneath it was the Trilon logo.

"Ms. Gomez?"

Nellie tore herself away and ducked into Dr. Callender's office. He was a small man with stylish glasses and a thick head of dark brown hair.

"Sorry to keep you waiting," he said. "Meeting with pharmaceutical reps is sadly necessary. How can I help you? You wanted to talk about Mr. Cahill."

"Yes, I need to know what's going on and I need to know now."

Dr. Callender held up his hands in surrender. "Of course," he said. "Mr. Cahill has gone through a very difficult time, a great deal of stress."

Nellie narrowed her eyes. "He's dealt with stress his entire life."

The doctor nodded his head sadly. "Sometimes the ones who seem strongest are most at risk. They take the world on their back, never imagining a time when they can't handle the weight."

"But what do we do? How do we . . ."

"Fix him?" Dr. Callender asked. "If only it were that easy. I'm trying different drugs and we're doing intensive therapy, but it's a matter of time."

Nellie felt a sinking sensation. "Are you saying it's possible that he'll . . ."

"Stress is an insidious thing, Ms. Gomez," Dr. Callender said. "It's nearly impossible for us to ever really know its effects, or, once the effects take hold, the long-term outlook. As you said, though, Mr. Cahill is very strong. I'm optimistic."

Nellie nodded, numb. She rose from her chair, still in a daze. "Thank you for your time."

She stumbled out of the office and into the bustling hallway. "Sorry," she said as she made her way through the nurses and visitors. "Excuse me."

Thoughts of Fiske quickly turned to Amy and Dan. Was Fiske a vision of their future? Would a life of stress and danger break them, too? Nellie shuddered. Her kiddos had never felt so far away.

A laugh down the hall caught her attention. The woman in the red blazer came out of another doctor's office. She waved and then headed down the hall in the same direction Nellie was going, her spiked heels click-clacking against the linoleum. Her purse hung by her side, the key card with its large red A swinging back and forth.

Nellie squared her shoulders, her eyes locked on the key card. She couldn't be at Amy and Dan's side right now because she had a mission to complete.

Nellie started down the hall, praying her back was stronger than Fiske's.

CHAPTER 23

Spitsbergen Island, The Svalbard Archipelago

Amy's entire world was snow. She sank into it with every step and it blew so thickly through the air that Amy could barely see five feet in front of her. Not that there was anything to see. She had been walking for at least an hour now and the landscape around her was still nothing but fields of white, broken now and again by a gray pillar of rock.

Amy pulled a GPS device from the pocket of her heavy coat and wiped the snow off its face with her thick gloves.

Her position was marked as a blue dot moving slowly across the face of Spitsbergen, an island in the middle of the Arctic Ocean. It was part of Norway's remote Svalbard territories and sat within the Arctic Circle, less than seven hundred miles from the North Pole. Her dot was creeping along the road that connected the Longyearbyen airport, where she had landed only hours ago, to the Svalbard Global Seed Vault.

As small as the airport was, she could have gotten a

taxi to take her to the vault. The pilot had gone to great pains to point out that while the thermometer claimed it was a balmy two degrees out, the winds would radically increase her risk of hypothermia, cold weather gear or not. Amy wasn't about to take chances on a driver, though. The media might have already broadcast her location across the world. If they had, she was sure that Pierce's men wouldn't miss an opportunity to arrange a little accident for her, and she couldn't let anyone else get involved. As difficult as it made getting into the facility, Amy was relieved when she learned the seed bank was only staffed twice a year to accept new seed shipments. There wouldn't be another soul at Svalbard for months, and that meant there was no one she could hurt.

The screen of the GPS pulsed. She was almost there. The snowfall wavered in the wind and Amy caught sight of an undulating glow in the distance. She dropped the GPS into her pocket and trudged the last hundred yards up a rocky hill. Amy moved carefully, half bent over, gloved hands grasping rocks and her thick boots kicking into whatever crevice she could find. Finally, the jagged land gave way to a flat road covered by a thick sheet of snow.

Amy could just make out the gray lines of the entrance to the Svalbard Global Seed Vault. It was a simple steel rectangle, about twenty feet high, standing at the edge of the road like an immense burial marker. A square at the top of the monolith glowed in shifting patterns of turquoise and blue. Amy had read about it on the flight over and learned that it was meant to evoke the skies above the Arctic Circle.

A steel corridor ran from the facility's entrance into the snowbank behind. Beyond that, the structure plunged into the sandstone of the mountain, tunneling through nearly four hundred feet of solid rock before it branched off into the refrigerated seed storage areas. That they would need to refrigerate anything out here seemed insane to Amy, but it was to keep the seeds at a constant zero degrees. The idea was that the stored seeds would act as a kind of backup system for every plant on earth. If some tree in the middle of the jungle suddenly went extinct, no problem; with the seeds stored in the vault they could bring it back. They must have been thrilled to receive the silphium. A plant brought back from the dead!

Amy pulled a pair of binoculars from her backpack and scanned the area. The snow along the roadway and by the door was fresh powder, unmarred by any tracks. She checked the road behind her. No sign of Pierce's men there. A few buildings sat a mile or so to the south, but Amy didn't see any light coming from them. Amy wished all the isolation could put her mind at ease, but she knew how good Pierce's men were. If they didn't want to be seen, they wouldn't be.

Amy pocketed the binoculars and crossed the road, leaning into the wind. Once she was at the entrance she brought out a handheld computer with a series of wires running to a key card. Amy slid the card into the reader on the door and the machine went to work. Soon there was a click and the door opened. Amy peered down the hallway on the other side. She looked for tracks inside the door, signs that someone had been there, but the floor was clean.

Amy pulled the door closed behind her, filling the gloom with the fog of her breath. She was out of the wind, but it was no warmer inside the facility. Luckily, she wouldn't have to be there long. The seed vaults were about three hundred feet dead ahead, sealed off behind blast doors. Just to the right of the vaults was a small office for the staff. That's where she was going.

Amy crept down the hallway with her nerves on high alert. She was painfully aware that she was in the perfect place to be ambushed. If Pierce's men hit her now, there would be no escape and no witnesses.

The office was nothing more than a few desks and chairs with computers. A thermostat sat on one wall but there was no point turning the heat on. She'd be in and out before it even kicked in. Amy stripped off her gloves and hit the power button on the nearest terminal. The computer screen filled with unfamiliar icons and text in Norwegian. Not that it mattered. All she had to do was get online and download a program from a site Pony set up back in Attleboro. Once she did, the screen pulsed green three times and then a glowing green skull appeared along with the words *YOU. HAVE. BEEN. PWNED!!!*

Amy rolled her eyes and waited until the skull vanished, replaced by a green cursor.

Connected. Amy typed and hit SEND.

Minutes ticked by as she waited for a response. Amy cupped her bare fingers over her mouth and blew, eager for any bit of warmth. *Come on, Pony. Where are you?*

She glanced out into the hallway. It was empty but her pulse began to thump anyway. The quiet was intense, like being at the bottom of the sea. She could feel the entire mountain pressing down on her shoulders. Amy almost jumped when the computer pinged.

What's up?

"He may be a genius," Amy said out loud. "But his memory could clearly use a little work."

The vault doors, she typed, with fingers already going stiff from the cold. *Remember? You need to hack the system and find out where the silphium is, then open the vault door so I can get to it?*

Right! Of course! I'm on it.

Pony returned a moment later. *Vault #1-Row #8-Bin #63.* There was a metallic *ka-chunk* out in the hallway. Amy peeked outside as one of the blast doors swung open.

You're the best, Pony! Amy typed, but there was no response. That boy seriously needed to work on his social skills.

A blast of cold air hit Amy as soon as she stepped into vault number one. It was like standing in the middle of a supercharged freezer. Her breath rose in billows of white and the skin on her hands and face burned with the cold. Amy pulled her gloves back on and tightened the insulated hood across her face. *I just have to get in and out,* she thought.

The vault itself was as big as a football field, with thirty-foot ceilings. Blue shelving units ran the length of the floor and all the way up to the ceiling. Each one was packed with row after row of gray plastic bins.

Amy found her way to row eight and then ran its length until she came to bin sixty-three. Inside there were scores of aluminum packets, each one marked with the name of the seeds inside. Her cold fingers fumbled with the slick envelopes until she found what she was looking for. Amy pulled out the packet and held it up to read the label: *Silphium. Five (5) seeds.*

Gotcha, Amy thought.

"That was quite a stunt you pulled with those reporters."

Amy whipped around to find a man standing at the end of the aisle, leaning casually against the shelves. He was tall and broad and dressed all in black gear, which made his shockingly blue eyes stand out all the more. Amy hid the silphium packet behind her. Her muscles tensed, ready to run.

"Luckily, we're pretty adaptable," he said with a shrug. "Traveling lighter now so we don't raise any media eyebrows. Adapt or die. That's the rule, right?"

The refrigeration units kicked on again with a loud blast of air, and the man turned. Amy exploded off the floor, swinging her backpack hard as she ran straight at him. It struck the man on his shoulder, taking him by surprise and knocking him back long enough for Amy to speed past him, arms pumping. The door was in sight. She'd be out in seconds and then she'd—

Amy hit what felt like a brick wall and went flying backward. She slammed into the floor and the package of silphium shot across the concrete. Another one of Pierce's men stepped through the door, crossing his arms over his enormous chest.

The blue-eyed man laughed as he walked up behind Amy. "I said we were traveling lighter. You didn't think that meant I was dumb enough to come all the way out here alone, did you?"

The mercenary by the door reached for the gun on his hip, but the blue-eyed man waved him away.

"Go get the truck."

The massive man faded back into the corridor. Wind howled as the outer door opened and closed. The blue-eyed man took the package of silphium off the ground as he approached her.

"Why would you come all the way out here for a package of seeds?"

His eyes bored into Amy, but she said nothing. The man shrugged and tore the package open, upending it so the seeds fell out onto the concrete floor. He lifted his boot over the pile.

"No!" Amy rushed to stop him but it was too late. His boot heel fell. When he lifted it again, the seeds had been ground to dust.

Amy stared at the powder, a dark chasm yawning open inside of her. The next thing she knew the man grabbed her by the ankles and pulled her toward him. Amy struggled, but he was too strong. He held her down with one hand while he systematically stripped off her cold weather gear with the other.

"Now, let's try and think of a good headline," the blue-eyed man said as he gathered her gear into a ball and stuffed it into her backpack along with her phone and the rest of her supplies. "How about, *Internationally Known Troublemaker Vandalizes Famed Landmark Only to Get Trapped and Freeze to Death*."

"You don't have to do this," Amy said as the man slung her pack over his shoulder and headed toward the door. "Please, listen to me. You can't—"

The door slammed shut behind him. Amy leaped up and threw herself at it, pounding on the steel as the locks fell into place. "Wait! Please!"

The outer door closed with a deep boom and then there was silence. Amy slid down the length of steel door and hit the ground. The refrigeration system kicked on again, sending fingers of icy wind in all directions. The man had left her in a thin sweater and thermals. No coat. No hood. No gloves. No snow pants. She could feel her skin freezing and then the cold sinking deeper, reaching out for bone. Amy wrapped her arms around herself as she looked across the concrete-and-steel vault that would be her tomb.

CHAPTER 24

Amy got to her feet and walked the perimeter of the vault, shivering as she examined every corner of her prison. She felt a moment of excitement when she found a refrigeration duct within reach. Maybe she could crawl through it and out into the main office, where she could crank up the heat. But that dream was dashed. The slotted steel cover on the vent was bolted down, and her freezing fingers couldn't so much as budge it.

Another burst of hope came when she discovered a computer terminal fixed to a back wall, but all it seemed to do was search the seed database. It had no control over the doors and wasn't connected to the Internet.

Amy fumbled with the mouse next to the terminal and started clicking through menus in Norwegian, her hands so cold she could barely control them. She stumbled upon a map of all the computers inside the facility. There were notations for three computers sitting in a row, which must have been three terminals inside the vaults, and then four together in a separate location. Those must be the office! Amy had to use her palm to move the mouse. Her hands were growing more and more numb, making her fingers thick and heavy. She rubbed her hands together and tried again, clicking on each computer in turn until her screen went black and a small green cursor appeared at the bottom. Got it!

Pony! she typed. *911. Emergency. Trapped in the vault. Need help!*

Amy hit SEND, then stood back from the computer, hugging herself and stamping her feet to fight the cold. *Come on, Pony. Come on.* The refrigeration cycled on again, sending a cruel blast of freezing air over her body. Tremors shook her arms and shoulders.

Amy knew she couldn't stay still any longer, she had to get her body temperature up. She moved away from the terminal and started jogging around the shelves, her white breath trailing behind her. As she ran, Amy worked through every escape she had made over the last few years. How many hopeless situations had she found her way out of at the last second? A hundred? More? One of them had to have something in common with where she found herself now, one of them would offer her a solution, an escape. But every scenario she came up with hit a wall. Why? What was the difference between now and then? In answer, a single word dropped into her mind.

Dan, she thought. *He was the difference. Dan and Jake and Atticus and Ian and Hamilton. I wasn't alone then.*

Amy pushed the thought out of her head. Having other people here wouldn't make the vault any less escape-proof, all it would do was get the people she loved killed alongside her. Amy forced herself to take another lap around the vault. She could feel how much slower she was already. Her legs felt thick and numb, and the cold seared her lungs with every breath.

As Amy came back around toward the computer terminal, she stumbled and went crashing into the concrete. She got her hands under her and pushed, but the cold was creeping into her arms. *Come on, Cahill*, she insisted. *Push yourself up. You can do it.* Amy strained, but her arms were shaking so badly now that the best she could do was throw herself onto her side and then slowly curl up to a seated position, with her back against an icy wall. The terminal was just a few yards away. The screen was black, nothing but her own words mocking her on the screen.

Amy pulled her knees up to her chest, hugging them close to her chest, trying to trap every degree of heat. The shivering was growing more intense, almost like convulsions now. She tried to still it, but it was no use. She felt as if she were trapped within a fist of ice. The tips of her ears stung badly, as if a small creature were gnawing at them with needle teeth. Most alarming were the itchy spots of red growing along her fingertips. It was the beginning of frostbite. In a short time, her skin would harden and blister. Then the red would turn to black, and her fingers would be gone.

Amy tucked her hands in her armpits and dropped her forehead to her knees. She wondered where Dan and the others were right then. Maybe swimming in the Mediterranean? She could almost feel the warmth of the water and the weightless feeling of floating in it, under that intense blue sky. Amy's eyelids began to droop and she felt a strange sensation in the back of her mind, like the approach of a dark storm front. It wasn't frightening, though. In fact, Amy could tell that when the mass of roiling black clouds finally overtook her, she would feel calm and at peace. She would simply drift away.

A voice in the back of her head urged her up, reminding her that Pierce was still out there, that she had to stop him, but that voice seemed to grow fainter and fainter. Soon it was little more than a whisper.

Amy's hand slipped and hit the concrete with a bony crack. She hissed in pain, then tried to lift it again, but it was so heavy. Her whole body was. She had never felt so sleepy. Maybe if she rested for a little while . . .

There was a metallic ping somewhere far away. It was muffled, like a bell wrapped in layers of cotton, but it persisted. At first the sound was only a tiny prick against Amy's skin, but it sank in like a hook, dragging Amy up through layers of darkness. The ping grew louder. Something in the refrigeration ducts? Amy gritted her teeth. One ping every few seconds. Amy got her eyes open a slit and searched the vault. The ping sounded again and this time she saw the computer screen brighten as it did.

A flare lit inside Amy and she seized it before it went out. She began to move, slow and dumb, each turn of her joints a rusty torment, but she was moving. She dug her spine into the wall behind her and flexed her legs until she began to rise. She made it up, trembling, and planted a palm flat on the wall. She staggered forward, the whole time feeling like there was an anchor attached to her chest, trying to pull her down. Amy kept her eyes locked on the computer, and her brother's image fixed in her mind.

The computer pinged again.

"Coming," Amy said, her voice slurry and indistinct. "I'm coming. . . ."

Amy collapsed into the wall beside the computer. A message flashed on the screen. *What's going on? Where are you?*

Amy lifted her hands to the keyboard. The red splotches covered her fingers now and were creeping up to her knuckles. Her hands were as numb as lumps of clay. She lifted one hand with the other and set a finger down on key after key.

Valt 1. dor lcked. Need u to opn

Amy mashed ENTER, then slumped against the wall beside the terminal, staring at the blinking cursor until her eyes closed again and the dark pulled at her. The refrigeration system roared again, sending icy needles into the air. *Hurry, Pony,* Amy thought as her eyes drooped. *Hurry.*

There was a click across the room. Amy's eyes snapped open and she turned toward it. The door was open. Amy pushed off from the wall, reeled across the space, and threw herself into the hallway.

The office. Pierce's men had smashed the computer monitors before they left, but she didn't care about them. Amy crashed through the desks until she got to the far wall and reached for the thermostat. Her fingers hit shards of glass and broken plastic. Wires hung uselessly from the wall.

. . . troublemaker vandalizes famed landmark . . .

Amy turned away, a sound bubbling up inside her, something between laughter and a sob. The animal strangeness of the sound terrified her. She lurched away from the wall, trying to get her thoughts in order. *They needed to make it look like an accident,* she thought. *Like I came here and got careless. Maybe that means they left behind . . .*

Her backpack sat on one of the tables and her coat hung from the back of the chair. She fumbled with the coat, able to summon enough strength to get her arms through it and lift the hood, but not enough to work the zipper. The two sides of the coat hung limp, away from her body, nearly useless. She jammed her frozen hands into the gloves, expecting a surge of warmth now that she was dressed, but none came. Her body was so cold that the coat and gloves had no heat to trap.

Amy went for her backpack next but wasn't surprised to find that her phone was gone, along with all of her other supplies. Her frozen hand hit a padded envelope, and it was like a tuning fork was struck inside her. She pulled it out and opened it. Sammy's vial of serum was tucked inside. Amy stared at it as she shivered. One drink and she could probably sprint back to the airport but she knew the serum wouldn't just save her. It would make her into a monster, too. A monster like Pierce.

Amy thrust the serum into the pack and made it back out into the corridor, pulling herself toward the outer door. The hallway offered shelter, but it was still so cold inside that all it would do was kill her marginally more slowly. If she wanted to live, she needed to find help. Fast.

Amy threw her shoulder into the door, digging her feet into the concrete until the door gave and she fell out onto the roadway. She hit the ground hard and rolled, tipping over the edge of a hill and tumbling down an embankment. Outcroppings of stone struck her back and arms as she fell, but with the numbness she barely felt them.

Amy hit bottom and lay puffing on her back, the wind blowing across her body, carrying away any scrap of heat she had left. *Have to keep going. Keep moving.* She made herself roll over and climb onto her feet. It was night now and the snow was swirling around her, a white fog in the blackness. When Amy turned around, she couldn't even see the vault entrance or the aqua glow of its marker.

The wind howled in her ears and bit at her body. Though most of the landscape had been wiped away, Amy could make out a flat depression in the white, like a ribbon that ran down and around the mountain. A road? But to where? Amy felt sure she knew, but her brain was running as thick as sludge and no answer came.

Amy turned south toward an outcropping of dark structures down the hill. They appeared and disappeared in the drifting snow but she was sure she made out walls and roofs. Surely she could reach them and then someone would help her. Take her in. Just like Bhaile Anois. Everything became perfectly clear in an instant. And now that she looked at the buildings more closely, the buildings weren't dark at all, were they? There were lights on, warm amber lamps glowing in the windows and the doorways. And couldn't she smell the woodsy plume of chimney smoke and cooking fires? She could hear the warm din of voices, all talking excitedly over one another.

The sounds reached into Amy and pulled. She yanked her foot up out of a shin-deep drift and got moving. Her pace was agonizingly slow as she fought the snow and the darkness and the wind striking her with all its force.

Amy pulled a last bit of strength from the wispy

images of all her friends waiting for her down below. Dan. Atticus. Jake. Ian.

Evan.

Amy's mind hitched at the name, struck by the strangeness of it. A nagging voice in the back of her mind told her that Evan couldn't be there, but she didn't know why. How could Evan be gone when his face was so clear in her mind? When she could hear his voice, as clear as if he was standing right beside her? Amy lowered her head into the wind and marched through the snow, the promise of seeing Evan like a fire, urging her onward.

Time passed strangely, stretching and contracting, speeding up and then slowing to a numbing crawl. Amy barely even felt the cold anymore. Her body didn't shake. In fact, a strange warmth was growing in her. Her gloves fell off her hands and her coat slipped from her shoulders and dropped into the snow. She left it behind and continued on. She didn't need it anymore. She would be home soon.

Eventually, the snow stopped and the clouds retreated. Above Amy, stars glittered hard in the black. The white landscape stretched out before her, clean and still. Her foot struck something hard and Amy threw her hands out to keep from falling. They touched wood. Amy looked up and saw dark timbers stretching into the sky. Rough planks stretched to either side. A wall.

Amy reeled forward into a wide doorway, fully expecting to see Grace and Dan and the others waiting for her, and to smell food cooking. Instead she found herself in an empty room covered in ivory sheets of snow. The floors were white. The walls were draped in it. Amy craned her head back and looked up. The roof was riven with gaping holes. She could see the stars through it.

Amy fell backward and struck ground without any pain. She sank deep into snow so soft it felt like a feather mattress. She felt herself float, weightless and dreamy, looking up at the dark sky. Some part of herself told her to get up, keep moving, but the voice was faint and her body wouldn't listen anyway. Every part of Amy was retreating deep within her, forming itself into something wrinkled and hard, like a seed or the stone buried in a piece of fruit. Her body became a shell, thick and unfeeling. The world fell away except for the distant whispering of air from somewhere high above.

"Amy! Amy, can you hear me?"

It was Dan. He was standing right beside her, looking exactly as he had when she left him. Amy used every ounce of her strength to reach out to him, but her hand only brushed air.

"I'm okay," she croaked. "I found Bhaile Anois."

There was a flash of white light and Amy was weightless, rising out of the snow. Dan was gone now and it was Jake at her side, gliding along, his lips moving without sound, his hand wrapped around hers. There was a gust of wind and Jake became Evan and Evan became her father and then her mother. Amy felt her heart turn painfully. She was so happy they were here. So happy to be going home.

CHAPTER 25

Cara closed her laptop, settling her aching body into her executive chair. She had been training nonstop for her next bout with Galt and was feeling it.

Down the hall, the door to her father's study opened and slammed shut. Galt had gone in hours ago. Since then, all Cara had heard was murmuring voices interrupted by spikes of laughter.

Laughing at me.

Ever since her defeat in the gym, her father had been spending more time with Galt while she was stuck helping out with her mother's annual teddy bear inventory. If she had to count one more bear, she felt sure she'd scream.

There were footsteps as Galt and her father went to their separate rooms, shutting the doors behind them. The house settled into quiet. Cara left her room and wandered in the dark. She moved from the kitchen and through the den to the open doorway of her father's empty study. When she and Galt were kids, they would test each other's courage with escalating dares. *I dare you to touch his door and come back. I double dare you to step one foot inside.*

And now Galt went in and sat down behind closed doors and had hours of conversations while she was shut out. *Why him?* Cara racked her brain.

Because he beat me. Because he's faster. Stronger. Smarter. Better.

The realization hung on her shoulders like a sheet of lead. Cara left her father's study and headed back to her room. Maybe if she slept on it, she would feel a little better in the morning. She stopped and jumped back at the sound of someone else moving through the house. It was her father. What was he doing in the kitchen at this hour?

Her father clicked on an overhead light and reached into a cabinet. He pulled down a juicer and various powders, and then the family's protein shake bottles.

He's making our morning shakes, Cara thought. *He's been giving us these things for ages, and I've never actually seen him make one.*

He started by juicing a number of different fruits and vegetables: apples, grapes, peaches, broccoli, kale, some strange-looking grass. He poured equal amounts of each juice mixture into each bottle, followed with a scoop of protein powder. Then he took something out of the pocket of his robe and held it up into the light.

It was a squat glass vial, full with a thick-looking greenish liquid. Her father took a syringe out of his pocket and tore off its sterile wrapper. He plunged the syringe into the vial and filled it with the liquid.

Cara looked on, shocked. *That's not protein powder,* Cara thought. *That's a drug! What's he doing?*

Pierce held the needle tip over Galt's bottle and carefully pressed the plunger. A long stream of the drug shot into Galt's shake. When the needle was empty, Pierce shook the bottle vigorously and put it in the refrigerator. He turned to Cara's bottle next, but this time he filled the syringe less than halfway before squeezing it into Cara's shake. He capped her bottle, shook it, and put it in the fridge next to Galt's. Once the kitchen was spotless, he hit the light and left.

When she heard the door to Pierce's bedroom shut, Cara crept toward the refrigerator. She pulled the bottles out and set them down on the counter, feeling her rage build as it all became clear.

Galt wasn't better than her. He wasn't stronger or faster and he certainly wasn't smarter. He was cheating! Worse than that, her father was cheating for him.

Cara stood quietly for a while, staring at the bottles. Then she grabbed hers and worked a fingernail beneath the label. She switched her label with Galt's so she got the full boost and he got the scraps.

What will it be like, Cara wondered, *to feel all that strength? To show Galt once and for all who's number one?*

Cara's stomach knotted with anger, and a strange sort of hunger.

Let's see who the fittest is now, Dad.

CHAPTER 26

Amy woke in a half-lit room, bleary, her body as heavy as a sack of concrete. There was a strange tearing sound in the air, like paper being ripped again and again. Her muscles ached as she pushed herself up. She was in what looked like a generic hotel room, white and beige walls, big-screen TV, shaded windows.

"You're in Oslo."

Dan was sitting at a desk across the room. As she turned to him, a scrap of paper fell from his hands into a trash can by his feet.

"How . . . ?" Amy began, recoiling from the pain of what felt like ground-up glass in her throat.

"The boat captain got Attleboro on the radio," he said, his voice a flat line. "They sent a helicopter to pick me up and then I came to get you."

"So you really were there," Amy said, almost to herself. "That was you."

"If we'd gotten there a few minutes later, you would have been dead."

Instead of relief in Dan's voice, Amy thought

she heard something harder, like an accusation. Her arms were weak but she managed to haul the down-filled comforter off. She recoiled at the sight of herself. Her legs were covered in ugly purple bruises and so were her arms and her side. The tips of three fingers were numb beneath white bandages.

"We need to get moving," she said, trying not to groan as she pushed herself to the edge of the bed. "We can still get the seeds in Tunis. Maybe if we—"

A plastic bag rattled as it flew across the room and landed on the bed. It was full of small tan seeds. She looked up at Dan. "How?"

"Atticus and Jake got a plane to Tunis. They tracked the seeds down through their dad's friends."

"Everyone's okay?"

Dan said nothing. Just nodded. He wasn't even looking at her.

"Dan—"

"Explain how you could do something so completely insane!" Dan said, exploding out of his chair, his face red with anger. "Do you have any idea how worried all of us were? You could have gotten yourself killed!"

"I did what I thought was best," Amy said, trying to control what was building up inside her. "I'm the leader of the—"

"Don't give me that 'leader of the Cahills' junk!" Dan yelled. "We work *together*! We always have. Everything good we've ever accomplished, we accomplished together!"

"Then why are you leaving!?" Amy's cry felt like it was ripped from the very center of her. It battered the walls of the small room. "I saw those brochures, Dan. The ones you've been hiding from me. What? It's okay for you to go off on your own but not me?"

Dan's face was so red it looked as if it was burning. "I told you, I was going after this is over. *After.*"

Amy couldn't control the tears coursing down her cheeks. "This is never going to be over! You said that yourself. After we deal with Pierce, someone else will come along, and then there'll be someone else after that. If you want to leave so badly, go now!"

"Is that what you want, Amy? You want me to leave? Want all of us to leave? Didn't almost dying out there show you how crazy that was?"

Dan waited for a response, but it was a long time coming.

"You can't have it both ways, Dan," Amy said, her voice so quiet he could barely hear it.

Dan couldn't meet his sister's eyes. "I called Jake and Atticus," he said. "They're meeting us here in Oslo tomorrow. Once we make a plan, we're all heading to Guatemala. Together."

Amy wanted to protest, but she didn't have the strength. She nodded weakly. Dan reached into his pocket and tossed a new phone across the room and onto Amy's bed.

"From Pony," he said. "To replace the one you lost in the vault. He also wanted me to tell you he's sorry."

"For what?"

"He said there must have been something wrong with the network. He was waiting at his computer the whole time you were in Svalbard, but he never heard from you."

Amy frowned. "I don't understand. Pony's the one who got me out."

Dan shook his head. "He said he never heard from you."

"But that's not possible. If I wasn't talking to him, then who . . ."

Dan shook his head and started for the door.

"Dan, wait. Please."

He stopped with his back to her, one hand on the doorknob. Amy remembered the brochures in his bag, each one filled with boys his age, laughing and smiling. Carefree.

"Evan had so many plans," she said softly, a tremble in her voice. "Did you know that he and his dad were going to take a year off together after he graduated high school? They were going to go to South America and help build houses for people who needed them. After that they were going to go to meet his mom in China, because they always dreamed of seeing the Great Wall. They had no idea that—"

The words caught in Amy's throat, too big and too terrible to pass.

"I want all of you to be happy. You and Jake and

Atticus and all the others. I don't want this for you. I don't want this for *anybody*. But you should go right now, Dan, before it's too late."

Dan seemed about to say something, but he didn't. He opened the door and stepped into the hall.

"Dan, wait, I —"

The door closed behind him with a slap. The silence in the hotel room settled heavily on Amy's shoulders. She looked away from the door and noticed that Dan had dragged the trash can out from under the desk. She remembered the sound of tearing paper and got herself out of the bed and went over to it.

Inside, there was a crumpled ball of paper streaked with blue and yellow and candy-apple red. Scraps of paper blew out of her hand and onto the floor as she unfolded it, like the feathers of some small, brilliantly colored bird. Dan's brochures. Each one, with its bold colors and smiling, lighthearted boys, had been torn in half and then torn again.

Amy's heart broke, looking down at them. She knew part of her should have been glad, but suddenly the thought of Dan staying made her ache worse than the thought of him leaving ever had.

There was a soft ding behind her. Amy flipped over her new phone and saw an e-mail waiting to be read. It was from Jake. She stared at it for a long time, her stomach turning, before she finally worked up the nerve to click on it.

Amy,

I don't think there's much to say, or
anything that Dan probably hasn't said
already, but there's one thing I had
to get off my chest. First off, Atticus
and I are glad you're okay. We were all
pretty mad when you took off without
us, but that was because we were
terrified. None of us know what we'd
do if anything happened to you.

I want you to know that I'm not
going to stop trying to help you
fight Pierce. But I accept what you
said before you left and want you to
know that I agree. There was never
anything between us and there never
will be. Don't waste any more time
worrying about feelings that neither
of us ever had.

—Jake

Amy closed the e-mail and then sat without moving
for some time. She looked around at the stark walls
of the room, and for a moment she felt like she was
back in the vault, trapped and alone. Amy hit REPLY
and started to type:

Jake,

I only said what I did because if you knew how I really felt, you would have pulled that plane out of the sky before you let me go off alone. And I'd rather you hate me and live than die because you care. I couldn't forgive myself if you or Atticus were hurt. But I'm tired of lying. And the truth is, there's no one I'd rather fight with, no one I'd rather be infuriated by, than you.

Dan said that the best things any of us have ever accomplished, we accomplished together. That's true for me and you as well.

—Amy

Amy stared at the message, thinking of how Jake teased her on the beach in Tunis, and then his face as she boarded the plane.

She highlighted the e-mail and hit DELETE.

Once the e-mail was gone, she moved to her browser and typed in *Guatemala* and *Riven Crystal*. A long list of hits came up and she moved through them one by one, examining each, making lists of notes, losing herself in the research.

CHAPTER 27

Nellie crouched in the weeds at the edge of the Trilon parking lot, looking up at the dark building. There were four labs with lights still on. She waited, legs cramping, until the lights went off one by one. Soon the straggling scientists left the building and got into their cars.

Nellie slipped out of the ditch and ran across the parking lot in a low crouch, doing her best to avoid the pools of light streaming down from towering steel poles. There was a security station just inside the main entrance that was manned 24/7, so that way was out. Luckily, she had the building's schematics all but memorized. Nellie left the parking lot and came around the north side of the building, belly crawling underneath the first-floor windows just in case.

Nellie found the side door and pulled a set of lock-pick tools out of her back pocket. She eased the thin metal tools into the lock and closed her eyes as she dug around inside, judging her success by the vibrations coming back through the metal. She felt tumblers move out of her way one by one, but got stuck on the last. It slipped and slid out of her grasp and her hands went tense.

Nellie heard footsteps out in the dark. No doubt a guard on patrol. He was getting closer. Twenty feet away. Then fifteen. Nellie poured her whole concentration into the tools, twisting and turning them. *Come on. Come on.* A flashlight beam appeared. Nellie held her breath. Ten feet. Five. The final tumbler lifted and the lock clicked open. She threw her shoulder into the door as the guard appeared. She rolled inside, sticking out one hand at the last second to stop the door before it slammed against the frame. She held it there, listening until the guard was gone again. Nellie eased the door shut and then turned into the gloom of the building.

She was in a first-floor stairwell. To get back to the vending machine she needed to go up three flights and then wind through the corridors until she was on the far-west side of the building.

Nellie got moving, slinking up to the fourth floor, then peeking out the door until she was sure no one was coming. The hallways were half lit by safety lights, filling the string of labs and corridors with an eerie gloom. Nellie froze at every sound, her body going on high alert until she realized that it was simply the building settling or the air-conditioning cycling on. She had memorized the placement of the video cameras and took a long and winding route to avoid them.

It felt like it took her hours before she finally ended up back at the dead-end hallway.

The snack machine glowed in front of her. As she approached it, the glass front picked up her reflection. Nellie's skin went cold as she imagined the black machine was a huge mouth, poised to devour her.

Come on, Gomez, pull yourself together. It's just your imagination.

Nellie's hands shook as she pulled the stolen key card from her back pocket. She had definitely picked up a thing or two over the years. A subtle shoulder bump and the pharmaceutical rep she had seen outside of Dr. Callender's office had been distracted enough that Nellie could swipe her card without being noticed. Nellie ran it through the reader. There was a click and one edge of the snack machine popped away from the wall.

Nellie peeked around the side of the machine. There was now a sliver of space between it and the wall behind. She slipped her fingertips into the crack that had formed and pulled. The snack-machine door swung open easily and without a sound. On the other side was a narrow concrete staircase leading down into darkness.

Nellie swallowed a growing lump of fear in her throat and stepped into the black, shutting the door behind her. She stood there in the dark, her heart hammering, until there was a faint hum all around her and a series of dim fluorescent lights cut on all along the staircase. *Huh*, Nellie thought. *I guess you can be evil and energy conscious at the same time.*

Nellie descended the stairs, crossing switchback landings at each floor until she had descended five levels. There, she found a landing and a steel-jacketed door. The basement should be just on the other side. She swiped her A card in the reader by the handle and the door popped open.

Nellie peeked through the doorway. On the other side was a nondescript hallway with large picture windows running down its length. She didn't see any people or hear any voices.

Nellie moved into the hallway in a slight crouch, easing the door closed behind her. When she came to the first lab, she flattened herself against the wall and peered over her shoulder.

The lab was filled with racks of computers, tables, chairs, and a chalkboard that was covered in a confusion of symbols. There was another lab next door just like it. She came to a third lab and found glass tanks filled with a thick green liquid. Odd, lumpy shapes floated in the green, while bubbles of air streamed past.

The serum, Nellie thought with a chill. Her instinct was to bust inside and smash the tanks, but she needed to see the full scale of the operation. As Nellie started down the hall, a door swung open behind her and someone exploded out of an adjoining room. A hand fell over her mouth and she was yanked out of the hallway and into another room. Nellie moved without thinking. She spied a fire extinguisher on the floor and grabbed it and swung as hard as she could. There was a satisfying yelp of pain and her attacker crashed to the floor. She pulled the steel canister back for another swipe.

"Nellie! Please! Wait!"

Nellie stopped mid-swing. Below her she saw a tangle of black hair and dark eyes wide with fear.

"Sammy!"

The fire extinguisher clanked to the ground and Nellie dropped down beside him. He had fallen against a nearby table and was bleeding from his forehead.

"Oh, no. Oh, God. I can't believe I just—are you okay?"

"I'm fine! But what—what are you doing here?"

Nellie grinned. "I'm your own personal cavalry. I'm going to get you out of here, but first, I need to see what Pierce is up to. Can you walk?"

Sammy nodded and Nellie helped him up. She put her back to the wall and peered out into the corridor. The coast was clear.

Nellie and Sammy moved down the hall. Nellie's mouth went dry and the muscles in her legs quivered as she drew closer. Another window sat in the wall ahead, the biggest one yet. Nellie moved up alongside it, her back to the wall. She was surprised to find her heart racing. She turned slowly and looked inside.

There were no people anywhere that she could see, only a factory floor the length of a football field, filled with ranks of black machines. A conveyer belt ran along the room, connecting machine to machine. But what was on it? Nellie moved in front of the window and peered into a back corner. What she saw there made her blood go cold.

"He's really doing it," Nellie said, struck dumb at the idea.

Along the back wall were three massive glass tanks, each one nearly three stories high. They were empty, but she knew soon they would be filled with the same thick green liquid she had seen earlier. Hoses ran from the bottom of the tanks to the machines that ran the conveyer belts.

"He's mass-producing the serum," Nellie said.

"But why?" Sammy asked.

There were hoses at the ready to squirt the serum into vials, and belts waiting to whisk the vials away. Nellie could see hundreds, maybe thousands of empty vials, just waiting for Pierce to press the button.

"Because," Nellie said, her face grim, "he's going to build an army."

a b c d e f g h i k l m n o

p q r R s t th u v w x y z

ATTLEBORO CRIER

LATE FINAL

By Stacy Lellos

TIKAL, GUATEMALA – No longer satisfied with risking his own life, Dan Cahill has taken his daredevil stunts to the next level—literally! Sources spotted the reckless teen hanging off a zip line hundreds of meters above the ground. A witness saw "a number of men in dark suits chasing him afterwards, probably a private security firm his guardians hired to keep him out of trouble." Are these experts in over their heads trying to wrangle this menace to public safety?

SEE PAGES 2, 3, AND 7

TERROR UNZIPPED!

Daredevil Dan Endangers THOUSANDS